Confessions

FROM A

Studio Apartment

Brieanna Robertson

Whimsical Publications, LLC

Florida

Confessions from a Studio Apartment is a work of fiction. Names, characters, and incidents are the products of the author's imagination and are either fictitious or are used fictitiously. Any resemblance to actual events or persons, living or dead, is entirely coincidental.

To purchase the authorized electronic edition of
Confessions from a Studio Apartment, visit
www.whimsicalpublications.com

Cover art by Traci Markou
Editing by Janet Durbin

ISBN-13: 978-1-940707-74-7

Published by
Whimsical Publications, LLC
Florida

We chair danced for awhile, which is always easier—less limbs to worry about—and finally progressed to moving out onto the dance floor. My nerves had finally relaxed and we were laughing and being silly, what we usually did best. The two of us never had an issue making idiots out of ourselves.

Buzzed, Roseanne finally shouted over to me, "I'm really horny!"

I raised an eyebrow and shouted back, "Yeah, that makes two of us!" I hadn't had sex since I was married. I didn't believe in premarital sex. So, there was that. I was human, after all. If I was a guy, I'd have a permanent affliction with which blue was part of the title.

"But we're single!" she cried in despair.

And for some reason, that was hilarious. We giggled and high-fived one another like it was some kind of accomplishment. It was a true *Sex in the City* type moment.

We danced some more before Roseanne really did start to look like she was going to drop dead, and we hoofed it back to the hotel. Thankfully, it had stopped raining.

When we got there, however, I felt broody and restless, not yet ready to go to sleep. I glanced at the clock and, since it was still decently early, I told Roseanne I was going to go to the restaurant across the street and to go ahead and go to sleep. She did so and I headed over to Tommy's Joynt, a place that was embedded in my memories as much as my ex was. And, really, I think that was half the reason I wanted to go.

I had taken Roseanne there the night before because I knew she would like it, but I still felt like I had to confront the ghosts of my past by myself, and Tommy's Joynt had a lot of ghosts. People spend a lot of time fearing the ghosts that they think are real, the supernatural creatures from beyond, but to me, the real ghosts you should fear are the ones of your own making. The memories from another life that haunt you, that make it impossible for you to move forward or move back. I had been dealing with these kinds of ghosts since I'd moved into my studio. I had methodically eradicated a lot of them, but the ones from this place were some of the worst…because the memories were some of the best.

I went to the bar and ordered a Guinness, then sat at an empty table and pulled out a notebook I had brought with me. I felt like I was going to burst. I had too many indecipherable emotions swirling around inside of me and the only way to purge them was to write some kind of bizarre, obscure poetry. So I did.

I'm not really sure how long I sat in there. All I know is that no one bothered me, which I was grateful for, I got out some kind of depressing poem, I briefly contemplated how sad it was that I was sitting alone in a bar/restaurant writing poetry, and I came to a startling realization.

I was really tired of being alone.

As much as I had come to love my independence. As much as I loved these girl adventures with my BFF.

There was something missing.

Something I craved.

Part of my brain bounced back to my conversation with Chris, the conversation I had at the time been so desperate to avoid. I hadn't really thought about it up till then. I had still been too hurt, too raw from everything. Most people said that in order to get over a relationship that had gone south, you had to go out there and start dating again, much like the "get back on the horse when you fall off" analogy. But I wasn't like everyone. I felt too deeply. The scars had not just scratched the surface, they had gone all the way through. If it was possible to feel one's heart obliterated, that's what I had felt. I honestly hadn't thought I possessed one anymore. Not in a romantic capacity at any rate.

But I sat there, in the place I had gone with my ex so many times, and I remembered. I allowed myself to remember and I let those memories wash over me and through me with a bittersweet kind of recognition. I didn't run from them. What would be the point? What was done was done, and what would be would be. So I re-lived those things. Part of my heart smiled. Part of my heart cried. But for the first time in too long, I actually felt my heart again. And on the heels of that realization, came an epiphany.

I really wanted another relationship.

I was ready.

I wasn't broken anymore.

And this terrified me.

The Real Life Chronicles #1
Confessions from a Studio Apartment

To the ones who shared the ride with me.
And to you. My sunrise.

"People often say that this or that person has not yet
found himself.
But the self is not something one finds, it is something
one creates."
—Thomas Szasz

Also by
Brieanna Robertson

Serendipity Series

The Road Less Traveled
Better Than Chocolate
Dark Masterpiece
Paladin
Stage Presents

Stand Alone Books

Amaranth of the Wild Things
The One Inside the Looking Glass

Chapter One

Endings and Beginnings

It was snowing. So fitting that it should be on this, my final month in the home that had felt more mine than anywhere else I had ever lived except the house I had grown up in. Last night of the year too. So ironic. So symbolic.

I couldn't believe it had been four years. Four years since I had bailed out of my toxic marriage, desperate to find a place of my own and somehow make it work when I was only working severely part-time. Of course I had my mom telling me I could move home, and I knew it would be all right if I did. I got along fine with my family, and I had done exactly that for a six-month stint when I wasn't sure if I wanted to divorce my husband or not. But I didn't fancy the thought of cramming myself into my childhood bedroom, putting all my stuff into storage, freezing my ass off in the winter, fighting my dad for the bathroom every morning, and feeling like I'd gone back to being a teenager when I'd been living on my own for the last however-many years. Plus, I don't know, I just needed to know that I could do it, that I could stand on my own two feet, that I didn't need to rely on anyone. After spending the last five years feeling worthless, it was extremely important to me that I prove to myself that I wasn't.

I'm not sure what made me get on the Internet that day I found my place. A client of mine had known I was looking to move and had given me a website that students used. She knew I was broke as a joke and needed something cheap. I didn't need to move right away—the divorce was amicable and my soon-to-be ex wasn't forcing me to move out—so there was no need to look until it was absolutely necessary. Plus, every time I looked around at the nice two-bedroom, two-bath apartment I currently lived in, and looked back on what I had thought was going to be my life until I was old and gray, I had a severe bout of major denial.

But for whatever reason, I'd had this annoying, repeating thought in my head that day, and I got online to see what that link was all about. Almost immediately, I saw this studio apartment going for the kind of rent I'd be certifiably insane to ignore. And it claimed all utilities were included. At that point, I did the only rational thing I could do—I called up my mommy and told her she had to go with me to check it out...because obviously the thought of going by myself was horrifying. Then it would make all of this entirely too real.

So, a few days later, armed with a key and an address, my mother and I wandered down a seedy-looking alleyway in not the greatest part of town and opened the door to an apartment the size of a thimble...and that was being generous. I immediately felt my stomach sink.

"Well...it's...very small," my mom commented.

I tried to be optimistic despite my dread. I mean, I couldn't overlook the fact that the rent was fantastic and I made less than minimum wage at the moment. "Well," I said as I wandered around in desperate search for positives, "the kitchen is nice." The bedroom, however, was like something out of one of my nightmares. Smaller than my childhood bedroom I was so adamant to avoid, I had no idea how I was gonna shove a bed, a couch, my computer, myself, and three cats in there. Not to mention the closet was the size of a shoe box and the toilet looked like it was from the dark ages. And what in the world was that thing on the wall?

"Oh wow, it has radiators," my mom supplied. "I bet you anything this place used to be an old farmhouse and they turned it into four studios."

Joy.

"Well, is that thing...functional?" I muttered, staring at the contraption I had only seen in movies that took place in New York. "Like, is it safe?" Leave it to me to pick some place to live that would end up blowing me sky-high. That was just my luck.

My mom assured me that it should be fine, but I still had

a hollow feeling around my heart. I hemmed and hawed, trying to figure out if I could actually make this insanity work, and we locked the place back up.

"You know, this isn't the picture they showed online," my mom said randomly. "Which studio was the one in the picture? Is it for rent?"

I could barely process what my mother was saying as I had descended into yet another "I can't believe this is actually happening" moment. But by the time I registered her words, she was already marching around to the front of what had at one time been a whole house.

"Is this one for rent?"

I frowned and walked over to where she was peering into the next apartment's window. I squinted my eyes through the slats of the blinds and was surprised to see that the room I was looking at was rather large. It had obviously been the original kitchen and there was enough room in there that I could probably put my couch and TV. A small bit of hope stirred where that hole had been in my chest. "I don't know," I said in answer to my mom. I walked around to the front. "This is the one that was in the picture, but this isn't the number they listed."

"Let's go back to the property management company and see if we can look at this one."

Thank goodness for my rational mother because lord knows, at that point in time, I was about as irrational as they came. I was lucky I was functioning at all.

Turned out, the property management company had only listed the one apartment because they hadn't remembered they had two to list. Upon inquiry, the secretary had found that the bigger apartment was available also.

I took it as a sign.

Three weeks later, I was sitting in the oldest building I had ever seen, with half of my stuff moved in, eating a Bertolli's frozen Italian dinner—with the one fork I had brought from my old home—and drinking a glass of wine while I sat in a folding chair and watched *Under the Tuscan Sun,* a favorite movie of mine that suddenly seemed much too close to reality.

I was crying my eyes out. Right over my chicken linguine alfredo.

It was a low moment.

A week or so later, I had gotten myself all moved in. I'd gone to a pub crawl with my mom and asked her to spend the first night on the couch at my new place because I was seriously freaked out about my new neighborhood, the weird hoarder guy who lived in the duplex in front of me and started every other morning by shouting at the top of his lungs, "Let's go! Let's go! Let's go!" And the fact that I was flying one hundred percent solo for the first time in my life.

I felt ridiculous. Here I was in my mid-twenties, asking my mother to stay with me because I was a spaz. It was February, about two weeks after I'd signed the lease. It was cold, and I'd had to fight with my landlord to get him to fix the radiator, which hadn't worked at all upon my moving in. As I lay in my bed, listening to that radiator make a wheezy-whir noise every time it came on, I wondered what the hell had happened to my life. I thought to myself, there was no way I could ever make this rundown place, with it's crazy Alice in Wonderland style bathroom—it was seriously weird, with a sloping diagonal wall across from the smallest shower imaginable and a tiny, airplane-sized cubicle with just enough room for a toilet, its ugly as heck pinkish glue-on kitchen tile, cheap turquoise hotel carpet, and older than the nineteen hundreds bathroom sink—my home.

I tried my best to look on the bright side. It was all I really had at the moment. Especially since at night, I got blitzed on wine, watched old musicals, and sang to my cats. Hey, I'm not saying it was the best decision on how to cope with my life, but at the time, it was all I was capable of.

I tried my best to turn the thing I viewed as my holding cell into a home. I even invited my parents over one night for dinner. They'd had to bring and cook all the food, of course, but it's the thought that counts, right?

It had been raining. It was raining all kinds that winter. And as we tried to settle in and watch a movie, I noticed two things. 1—the outside power line was smoking. Like seriously smoking. And 2—my stoner neighbor in the apartment next to me was standing on his step, smoking a cigarette, and watching it happen like there was nothing at all to be concerned about. When I brought it to my parents' attention, my mom asked said neighbor if he'd ever noticed it before.

"Uh...yeah. It does that every time it rains," he said as he took another drag.

I wanted to smack him. Really? Great, so he stood there, every time it rained, and watched the power line pose a threat of electrocution to anyone who walked by if it eroded and split it half? What a half-baked idiot. Maybe he should go smoke some more pot and kill what few brain cells he actually had left.

I said as much, loudly, to my parents inside my living room, not realizing the walls and windows were paper-thin and he could more than likely hear every word I said. Woops. I was lucky he didn't slash my tires. Although, he did start smoking on the back porch more frequently so he didn't have to come in contact with me. That was fine. He irritated me anyway. He always woke me up when he banged his door against the hinges every morning when he got off graveyard shift, and he always flushed the toilet when he knew I was in the shower. He was a turd.

But I digress.

At any rate, a call to the fire department and a visit from the power company later, my power line was fixed.

And a few months into my living there, my sketchy job status was also fixed. So maybe I was working full-time as a housekeeper of all things. At least I had a job. I was paying my own rent and was stable, more or less. It was a small victory that felt like a giant one. Lean Cuisines and ramen noodles for dinner aside, I was making it on my own. It was something every college kid had to go through, and so maybe I'd skipped that part and had to go through it *after* the marriage thing. Whatever. The important thing was that I was going through it, I was finding myself, or at least starting on the journey to relocate where said self had disappeared to.

The truth was I had lost myself almost as soon as I'd gotten married young and moved out of state for several years. I didn't know if I'd ever find that person I had once been. At that stage, I felt like that was as insurmountable as climbing Mt. Everest. But I had to try.

Because I had nothing left. Nothing. Not the sham of a marriage I had based all my hopes on and not the deluded dreams of an idealistic little girl. I barely had me. Even I was, more or less, just a shell. Something had to give and start looking up, because I couldn't foresee myself getting much lower...

My phone beeped, bringing me out of my trip into the past. I turned away from the window where I had been watching the snowflakes fall and flopped down on my couch, retrieving my cell from the coffee table.

"Hey baby-cakes, hope your night is going well. Thanks for dinner. Miss you and hope you sleep well. Xoxo."

I grinned and sent a reply, sappier than his—I was always sappier than him—and sighed, leaning my head back against the couch cushions. Deaven. My metaphoric pot of gold at the end of the rainbow. The one who had managed to set me free and capture me all at the same time. The man who had been the end and the beginning of me.

I glanced toward the window again and watched the snowflakes drift. I was already feeling nostalgic. Some part of me felt the need to take a trip down memory lane, to remember what had brought me to this place. I needed to remember so I would never take for granted what I had. The journey was the important part, and this had been mine. I didn't care if I was a sentimental sap. I was me. Finally. After so long.

And I wanted to remember the crazy ride that had brought me here...

Chapter Two

Adventures in the Snow with Chris

So, my first love in occupation has always been English. Grammar and the sort. But I didn't want to teach it. Good lord, no. I didn't want to deal with a bunch of kids. That was like a recipe for an immediate panic attack. But I did do some freelance editing. And in my meanderings through that field of work, I had happened upon Christopher Carol—no, not *Christmas Carol,* though I'm sure he got that a lot—who was a brilliant literary teacher, writer, and editor himself. For a few years, we had entertained ourselves with writing scenes here and there online, exercises to help us with our craft and to entertain us. Over the course of such exercises, and a few visits back and forth across the country—where accompanying adventure and mayhem ensued—we had become more than best friends. The man may as well have been my little brother.

Unfortunately, the day he decided to fly in was during the worst snowstorm my city had seen in years, and he had been delayed at LAX for hours. When he finally did arrive, there was about a foot of snow, he had been sent in on some bizarre charter propeller plane, and the streets were ridiculously difficult to navigate.

Now, I'd already been in my little apartment for almost a year by this time. The first year had gone by in a blur of divorce papers and working, then coming home and staring at the TV. My mom would come over often, and we would have movie marathons of the silliest proportions, which I was grateful for. At the time, it was what had probably kept me sane.

But I was used to my place now, its quirks and oddities.

Despite the fact that right after moving in, one night in a sleep-induced moment of confusion, I had tried to get out of my bed to go to the bathroom and had tangled my feet in the covers. Not such a big deal, generally, but when you have nowhere else to fall but face-first into a bookshelf because you have so little space, and you almost knock yourself unconscious? Yeah, a big deal.

And I was used to my work schedule, which was slowly picking up more editing.

I was also *almost* used to being single.

Needless to say, I was more than ready for a friend to visit, especially one who had been there with me through the good times and the bad and who would understand where I was in my life more than anyone.

After getting Chris situated in my lair and showing him where he would be spending the better part of a week—on the uncomfortable couch—he informed me that he needed to go get his drink on. I could understand that. The man was two seconds away from taking a Xanax after his harrowing trip across country. The least I could do was show him a good time.

So we hit one of the better clubs in my city. It just so happened that at the same time, my city had decided to host the annual Santa Crawl, which was just what it sounds like. Hundreds of drunk idiots dressing like Santa and all his cronies in the city's most elaborate display of debauchery anyone had ever seen.

My friend just wanted to have a good drink. He was stressed. And I didn't have anything to offer him other than my customary wine, which he thought was nasty, and my occasional rum and coke. So, I text messaged my bartender friend in Huntington Beach, CA and asked him what he would suggest.

One rum and coke, two gold...somethings, and three kamikazes later, my friend still didn't have a buzz, and we had listened to two sets of the cover band at the club. Finally, my bartender friend had told me to give him a zombie and have that be the end of it. Okay...cool. He obviously knew what he was talking about. He was a bartender. A half an hour later, Chris was swaying to "Riders on the Storm" in a hazy stupor that made him look like he was trying to channel the spirit of

Jim Morrison himself. He could barely stand upright and he was leaning against my back, draping his six-foot-three frame over me while I tried to drool properly over the super hot guitar player in the band. Between that and the seven billion Santas pressing in on me from all sides, I started to get extremely claustrophobic.

"Chris!" I shouted at him with a well-placed elbow in his abdominal region. "Dude, stop leaning on me!"

He wobbled and muttered something completely incoherent.

I rolled my eyes and grabbed his wrist, guiding him out of the club. "All right, time to go home," I told him when we were outside and could actually hear one another. We'd taken a cab since it was continuing to dump snow, and I called for one to come and get us to take us back to my apartment.

He was still babbling once we were in the safe confines of the taxi, but I didn't mind as much because I was no longer being crushed.

"What did your friend give me? He drugged my drink," he murmured as he leaned back against the seat, his voice dazed-sounding and whimsical.

"*He* didn't give you anything, Chris. He's in California."

"No, he did it telepathically."

I raised my eyebrow at him and smothered the urge to guffaw. "He did it telepathically? Really?"

"Yes!" he said emphatically, raising himself back up into a sitting position with gusto. "I was totally fine. I'd only had like four drinks."

"Four?" I did guffaw at that. "Honey, you had a lot more than four drinks."

"I don't know what you're talking about," he slurred. "I only spent seventy dollars."

A ludicrous amount of money to spend on drinks when I only spent about fifty dollars a month on groceries. "Yeah, seventy dollars on kamikazes and zombies!"

"There was only one zombie," he protested, holding his finger up, then chuckled because he undoubtedly had a small moment of clarity where he realized how smashed he was. "I will tell you what," he continued, "you drink a zombie and you're not yourself anymore."

"No," I agreed, enjoying the role I played in our friendship of being a relentless tease, "you're a zombie."

He leaned back against the seat again and muttered, "I'm like on a totally different plane."

So now my friend was becoming an existentialist. "Oh yeah?" I encouraged.

"Yeah, I'm like...an extraterrestrial."

Who in the world could come up with this other than a writer? I mean, really? Even in drunk mode, his brain was operating on hyper-creative. "An extraterrestrial, huh? From where?"

"The tenth planet," he responded without pause. I had to admire his ability to think on his feet, even while drunk and slumped in a taxi.

"And where is that exactly?"

He sat up again and gave me a look that can only be equated to the stereotypical "sassy black girl." He snorted and waved his finger at me. "Somewhere you don't even want to go." All he needed was the finger snap. Almost immediately, he switched gears and leaned forward toward the front seat. "Hey," he said to the driver. "What is the weirdest thing that's ever happened in your cab?"

The driver—a grizzled, bearded guy—thought for a moment before replying, "Well, I had someone die once."

This successfully both freaked out and intrigued my friend, so much that I was happy we were almost home because he started shooting rapid-fire questions at the driver about a poor man who had apparently had a heart attack.

After I managed to drag him away from the cabbie, I headed toward the apartment with keys in hand, ready to get my exhausted and obliterated friend to bed. What a first night. Not only did he have jet lag, but he'd had a day from hell and had drank probably the strongest drink ever known to man— which had turned him into an extraterrestrial from the tenth planet. I'd be lucky if he ever came to see me again.

As I fumbled with the keys in the dark, trying to locate mine amidst the horde of housekeeping client ones, I realized Chris had vanished. He was no longer behind me. I spun in alarm and immediately spotted him lying in the snow in my courtyard, holding his cell phone up like it was some kind of flashlight.

"Chris!" I cried. "What happened?" I ran to help him,

thinking there was something sprained or broken.

"I don't know," he replied with that faraway voice again. He waved his phone back and forth as if mesmerized by the glowing blue screen. The white sky above coupled with the enormous amounts of white everywhere else made everything insanely clear for the middle of the night and his tall, dark-haired frame contrasted so greatly that it looked like the snow just had a black, Chris-sized hole in it.

I put my hands on my hips. "What are you doing down there?" I demanded.

He flailed a minute before his grand epiphany. "Oh my gosh, why is my ass cold?" he cried.

I burst out laughing despite my attempts to be a good friend and caretaker. "Because you're laying in the snow, you idiot!"

"Oh my gosh, when did it snow?" He was shouting so loud I was surprised none of my neighbors came out to investigate.

That was it. Two things: I was never listening to my bartender friend again, and I was outlawing zombies. At least with literature and English majors. It apparently had a bad effect on them.

"A long time ago!" I snapped, less amused and more afraid my friend was going to die of hypothermia. "Remember? Propeller plane? Get up!" I grabbed his arm and tried to yank him up. He threw snow at me. I screamed.

I might have left him there, but some rational part of his brain decided he probably needed to cool it. He stumbled inside after me, and I was happy when I finally got him seated on the couch.

"Are you gonna spew?" I queried.

He looked up at me. "No, I'm fine," he assured.

Given his state of mind over the last few hours, I was skeptical. "Are you sure?" I prodded.

He grinned. "Yes, I'm okay. Just go to bed, Mickaela."

I reluctantly did so, hoping he didn't vomit all over my red shag rug. That would *not* be fun to try and clean. Luckily, he didn't. And I went off to work that morning thinking he was going to chill at home and maybe check out a few local coffee shops.

When I got home, I was tired. I always was after cleaning

someone's gigantic house. And it was worse because I'd had to drive on the two-foot sheet of ice that had become the roadway. Upon entering my apartment, I saw a note from Chris saying he had gone on a walk and was going to check out a few of the thrift stores that were in my area. I didn't think much of it. He was an independent sort of guy. I was just glad he didn't have the hangover of the century.

I wandered to my computer to check my email before I did anything else, as was my custom, and while I was doing so, my cats decided to have some kind of reenactment of WWI in the bathroom. I shouted at them to stop, finished my business online, and then headed for the shower. There was nothing I wanted more than a hot shower after sweating my butt off for several hours over someone else's toilets and dirt.

The first thing I noticed was that my cats were nowhere near the bathroom. Which was a little confusing, but I ignored it. Cats were stealthy, after all. The second thing I noticed was that there was a giant dark shape in my shower stall that should not have been there.

I blinked at it for a second, and waited.

One heartbeat...

Two heartbeats...

"Boo!" Chris came floundering out of the shower in an attempt to be scary.

I reacted a little because it was reflex. "Oh my...what the?" I stammered, but I really wasn't startled. I huffed. "I thought you were my cat."

He started laughing.

"What are you doing hanging out in my shower like some sort of creeper?"

"I was trying to practical joke you! Were you even scared at all?"

"No," I grumbled. I shook my head. "You are ridiculous." One of the things I loved about Chris was his endless zest for life and all things fun and silly. He was like a big ray of sunshine and I could never have a bad time when I was with him. He had come to visit at the exact time I needed him to, given I was nothing but a surly grumpy-gus most of the time.

I may have stopped wallowing on the couch and singing to my cats, but I had only really gone from depressed to mildly depressed, and the parts of me that were no longer depressed had just seemed to fill with jaded snark.

"But I went to so much trouble," he whined.

I giggled. "Epic fail, dude."

He huffed a melodramatic sigh. "Fine...what are the plans for tonight?"

I shrugged. "Lemme get in the shower—which, by the way, you should be thankful I did not come in here pulling off my clothes while you were attempting to be sneaky—and then we can decide."

He chuckled and nodded. "Sounds good."

He went out into my bedroom and started blaring all kinds of the weird indie rock he liked on my computer and I showered and attempted to make myself look presentable. I stared at myself in the mirror as I styled my short red hair and wondered when I had started looking so haggard. Or maybe it wasn't so much that I looked haggard, but that's how I felt. And when I looked at my blue eyes, they just looked tired. I missed seeing the vibrance that had once been there. Heck, I missed *feeling* that vibrance. Now all I ever felt was exhausted.

As a general rule, I tried not to feel sorry for myself, but every once in awhile, I was taken aback at the unexpected turns my life had taken. Everything felt out of place and backwards. I didn't even know where I fit anymore. I had been a wife with the idea that that was going to be my role for the rest of my life. I had not gone into marriage with a temporary view. I never would have suspected that six years later, I would be divorced and living on my own in a studio apartment. And I certainly never would have expected that I would be working myself into oblivion because that was the only thing I could grasp onto that made sense.

I cleaned all day, came home, and edited all night. It was a routine that was safe. It was mine. It kept me from having any kind of social life, and thus, kept out anyone who could potentially hurt me. The only person I ever went out with on occasion was my ex-husband of all people. Yeah, how healthy was that in my healing process? But he was safe too. He was familiar. And I'd had so much of the unfamiliar and the unsafe lately that I couldn't even begin to comprehend anything outside of my self-erected wall of protection.

Chris knew it. Even though I didn't readily discuss such

matters, he knew it all the same because he knew me. And he said as much later that night as we took a stroll through my neighborhood, enjoying the crisp, white beauty of the blanketing snow.

"Mickaela, do you remember when we first met each other and I was always calling you for advice on my crazy, soap opera life?" he questioned.

I giggled and stuffed my hands deeper into my coat pockets as we wandered. "Of course I do. You always had a crisis back then." I glanced up at his profile, so much more masculine and mature than when I had first seen him, and smiled. "You know how proud I am of you and the choices you've made in your life?"

He looked at me for a second and grinned. "Thanks. Do you remember how you were always telling me to find the beauty in things? To not give up on things like love and hope, even though sometimes that's all I wanted to do?"

A lump formed in my throat as I guessed where this conversation was heading. "Yeah," I muttered.

He sighed. "Do you remember during one of our last writing exercises, I asked you why you always wrote love stories?"

I nodded.

"And you said that you wrote for others what you could no longer believe in. And I remember thinking how horribly sad that was."

I scowled and kicked at some snow. "Sorry," I snapped.

He stopped and turned to face me, putting his hands on my shoulders. "Mickaela."

I reluctantly looked up at him. The empathy in his brown eyes made the lump in my throat start to choke me and I wanted to escape this entire conversation as soon as possible. I didn't want to think about the person I had once been, the person I had lost—the person I was pretty sure my marriage had killed. Odds were, that girl was never coming back again. I wasn't full of light and optimism anymore. I was full of bitterness and sarcasm. And I liked it that way. My prickles kept people away.

And keeping people away meant I was safe.

"You have been through so much, and you always survive. I have always called you a phoenix because that's what you are. You rise from the ashes again and again, no matter what life throws at you. You tried everything you could to keep your marriage from failing. It was not your fault that it dissolved. When you said that thing to me, about writing for others what you no longer believed in, it killed me because there is no one in this world more deserving of love than you."

I felt like my chest was going to be crushed and hot tears burned my eyes.

"I know it hurts. Trust me, I've been there. You know I have. I shut down for awhile too, but *you* were always the one who told me I couldn't give up. I don't want you to give up either. There is someone out there for you."

Chris's kind words made my heart constrict, but I shook my head. "I can't even fathom the thought of ever being in a relationship again," I admitted quietly. "I don't ever want to answer to someone else again. I like being on my own, making my own decisions, doing what I want, and not having to worry about another person's opinion. I don't want to go back to having to run all my thoughts by someone else first, of wondering, 'if I do this, is he gonna get mad?'" I rolled my eyes. "No thanks." *And I don't ever want to go back to feeling like I am completely unwanted in a relationship where I am supposed to feel anything but that,* I silently added. I would rather have stayed alone for the rest of my life than ever go back to the loneliness of a relationship where I felt completely unloved and misunderstood.

"And that's totally understandable," he said. "I just don't want you to give up. I want you to at least be open to the possibility. I want that for you more than anyone because of who you are."

I gave him a wobbly smile and wiped at my eyes. I appreciated his loyalty and his care. And it meant more than I could express that he thought that much of me, but I could not comprehend ever leaving myself open for another lethal stab to my heart. As far as I was concerned, it had already been killed once, and I didn't foresee it "rising from the ashes" this time. Chris was probably the only man left in the world that I would ever totally trust.

I linked my arm through his as we started walking again. "How about I just marry you, huh?" I suggested, trying to make light of a topic that I just wanted to go away. I knew my joke was a safe one. Chris and I would never work as a couple. We believed completely different things and lived completely opposing lives. For as much as we had in common, our differences were enormous. Plus, we had only had one fight in our entire friendship, but it had been so bad that we hadn't spoken to one another in over a month.

He chuckled and squeezed my arm. "Love, I'd change my religion and even get over some of my greater phobias if it meant I could be with you."

I looked up at him, startled, and his enigmatic smile made me wonder just how serious he was.

"I feel like, if I ended up with you, I'd never have to wonder anything about love ever again."

Chris was a romantic. A hopeless one. His heart was the size of the ocean. It was what I adored about him. So few men were like that in the world. He also had a tendency to be attracted to people of the masculine persuasion over the feminine kind. So, you can imagine how much his statement shocked me.

And as we continued to walk through the winter wonderland of the creepy back alleyways surrounding my apartment, I felt grateful that despite everything, I had a family who loved me unconditionally and who was always there for me, Chris included. And my heart felt full knowing that he was a constant in my life I would never have to worry about losing.

"I love you, you know," I said to him randomly.

"I love you too, babe."

It was innocent. It was safe. But at that moment, the love I felt for him was more than my withered little wounded heart thought it could feel.

And somewhere in the back of my mind, I wondered if he was right.

Chapter Three

Steak Sandwich

My phone beeped again, always my reality check. Any memories I was having went on the backburner because Deaven was my reality.

I picked up my phone and checked the text. It was something dirty that was not suitable for repeating. I bit my bottom lip and my heart did the usual *th-thump, th-thump* up near my throat that it had been accustomed to doing ever since I had first met Deaven. And I'd first met Deaven when I had been eighteen.

I smiled when I remembered that. I couldn't even recall what kind of party I had been at, but I had grown up in a circle of friends, a pack of kids who all ran together, from age ten onward. There was this slightly annoying boy I had known. Not my friend exactly, but a good friend of my good friend. He irritated me, and I had ignored him for the most part through most of my childhood.

By age eighteen, I had next to no contact with that boy anymore, but I had randomly run into this kid who had held a better conversation with me than any of the kids my age could even hope to. Needless to say, I was intrigued.

Not only did I find out that he was fourteen—which is a gigantic chasm of an age difference when you are a teenager—but I also discovered that he was the brother of said annoying boy I grew up with. I hadn't even known that kid had a brother. I spent my time that evening talking with that blond fourteen-year-old, and playing basketball with him. At that time, I'd been at an awkward age where I didn't really want to be around my "friends," because they all seemed super shallow to me, but I could not yet fit in with an adult conversation without getting weird looks. I had always been reluctant to grow up, but was told I was wise beyond my years, and something about that boy seemed much more mature than his age, so I had enjoyed hanging out with him, and I felt a connection that was surreal.

At the time, I'd been dating somebody. But the funny thing was, I had told my mother that I should just wait for Deaven to turn eighteen, because it was so obvious that I should end up with him.

Irony.

Enter a bar ten years later. I was actually with my ex-husband. Not *together*, together, but we were making a go of this "let's remain friends" thing, and he had finally convinced me to go out with him and his best man-friend. I was okay with it. After all, I wasn't looking for a...

Out of the random blue walked the kid from my past. He looked just the same, granted all grown up. And somewhere in the back of my mind, I remembered my words to my mother, as well as my thoughts during my conversation with Chris when he had said I needed to remain open for the possibility...

Possibility of what?

Some hidden part of me leapt to life and wanted to know. The dead cavern where my heart had once resided seemed to fill up with something it hadn't felt in longer than I could remember. I was pretty sure it was hope. All from one glimpse of a boy I had almost forgotten about.

I felt bad because I'm pretty sure my ex-husband was saying something to me, but I ignored him completely because Deaven and the man he was with decided to come and stand at the opposite end of our table.

Since I had already had a couple glasses of wine, I had bravery beyond what was normal, since I wasn't accustomed to being overly outgoing. I leaned over the table and said, "Hey, you're Deaven, right?" At his affirmative response, I said, "I don't know if you remember me. I met you ages ago. I'm Mickaela..."

I never finished my sentence because his perfect grin and bright blue eyes stole my breath, and his words, "I remember you," caused my heartbeat to falter. He remembered me? From one encounter ten years ago? Giddy teenage angst rushed back to me and we entered a conversation with no room for anyone else. Sorry, ex-husband. That probably seemed really rude, but at the time, I did not care.

We bantered back and forth for the better part of two hours, and when that time was finally up and I had to go home, I felt bereft. I kept texting the poor man, needing him to know how much I loved talking with him. This man understood my writing, my love of the written word and the arts, which I had discovered in my life, aside from Chris, was rare. He'd made me laugh more in one night than I think I had laughed in years.

As I walked up to my apartment door, ridiculously giggly, my good friend Roseanne, who had since moved in next door, came out and asked me what was going on.

I quickly gave her the rundown and she, true to her nature, told me she might vomit. I didn't care. I was deliriously happy. And even more so after I received his text message on my front step inviting me to dinner the next night.

Roseanne made even more gagging noises. I couldn't blame her really. She had just had a terrible break-up. I got where she was coming from.

But I went to sleep that night with the promise of seeing Deaven again, and at that moment, that seemed like winning the lottery...

Beep.

Back to the present I came once again. My phone was hot tonight. I glanced down at it again and grinned at the erotic text. Some of the romance authors I edited for would be jealous if they knew I was getting these kinds of text messages.

Too bad.

I fired off a response to my man and headed to the refrigerator for a snack. The pictures on the fridge door caught my attention and I smiled.

Deaven may have been the meat of my own romantic story, but none of it would have been half of what it was if not for some of the things in between.

Roseanne, for example.

I had known her since I was young. She was the daughter of my mom's long time friend who decided to move where we lived. The first several years of our relationship had been awkward for me. I didn't relate well to girls, and her statement of, "we are going to be best friends and have sleep overs!" when I had been thirteen had, needless to say, freaked me out.

So, we'd never actually had a sleep over as teenagers. In fact, I had stayed as far away as possible because Roseanne's overbearing personality, coupled with the fact that I had a difficult time getting along with most females, had made me feel that level of awkward no teen wants to feel. So, the few times I'd been to her house, I had spent the evening beating the tar out of Roseanne and her little sister at Mortal Combat. Hey, come on. All my guy friends were gamers. It was to be expected.

But over the years, we had grown as friends, and adulthood had bonded us like nothing else could have. We had failed relationships and the fact that we were now single on our side.

One night, while Roseanne had decided she wanted to go out and celebrate that very thing, we had ended up at my apartment after dancing our legs off and then eating Jack in the Box at three in the morning, which Roseanne declared was "the best cheeseburger she'd ever had."

We had dressed to the nines, wanting to feel hot and show off, and while I was trying to put on my pajamas, Roseanne was battling to get off her Spanx, and it looked like the Spanx was winning.

"Oh my gosh, I cannot get this thing off!" she cried as I watched, amused, at her flailing attempts to remove the spandex half-bodysuit. "I have to pee! This is really pissing me off!"

"Why are you trying to take it off in the kitchen?" I queried.

She stopped and gave me a look. "Well, because, Mickaela, I'm not exactly a size four and, if you haven't noticed, it's impossible for anyone larger than that to do just about anything in your kady-wompus bathroom." She took a great tug on her dress to get it over her head, sending her gigantic breasts all but spilling out, even while still in a bra. I blinked, not wanting to look, but unable to look away.

Her next move caused her to stumble and she went down on her knees, then started laughing so hard she rolled over onto her back.

I burst out laughing as she wriggled around on my floor, half-in, half-out of her Spanx and laughing so much she could hardly function. "What in the world are you doing?" I cried.

"I'm a turtle!" she exclaimed amidst belly laughs, squirming around on her back for effect.

I dissolved into laughter and tried to help her up, but was startled when someone knocked on my door. All laughter ceased and Roseanne and I looked at each other in confusion.

"Is someone at the door?" I asked stupidly. I glanced at the clock. "It's like three-thirty!"

"Here, gimme your hand." Roseanne pulled herself up and flung a robe over her half-dressed frame as she stalked to the door fearlessly. She pulled it open to reveal the neighbor from the duplex standing there, obviously drunk. "Hi," Roseanne greeted tentatively.

"Hey, girls, I just wanted to know if you wanted some steak sandwiches?"

I blinked and looked at the clock again for good measure, just to make sure it was, in fact, the middle of the night and I hadn't ended up in some kind of time wormhole. Nope. It was three-thirty. And he was apparently barbequing. Alrighty then.

"Um...no thanks?" Roseanne replied, sounding about as perplexed as I felt.

"Are you sure? There's more than enough and since I heard you guys come home and knew you were up, I thought I'd offer."

"Jack!" a female voice sounded behind him, followed by the crunching footsteps of shoes on the gravel in the courtyard. "Leave them alone! What are you doing?"

"I just thought I'd offer them some steak sandwiches!" he shouted back to his wife.

"It's the middle of the night! They probably want to go to sleep! Come on!"

"Are you sure?" he repeated, directing his attention back to Roseanne. "They're really good."

"Uh...we ate already, but thanks!"

"All right, well, if you change your mind..."

"Jack!" his wife shouted again, more insistent. "Come on, you're drunk!"

He muttered a good night and ambled off my front step. Roseanne shut the door and turned slowly to stare at me with a quizzical expression.

I laughed. "Yeah, that's Jack," I stated.

"And he's making steak sandwiches at three a.m. why?"

I shrugged. "I don't think he sleeps, like, at all. He's nice enough. Just weird."

"Everybody in this neighborhood is weird," she remarked, tugging off the rest of her Spanx and managing to get into her pajamas.

I snorted. "True enough...hey, the apartment on the end just opened up. You should move in there. You'd fit right in." I'd meant it as a jibe, but a spark of something came to life in her eyes.

"You know, that doesn't sound like a half bad idea. I'm about ready to strangle my roommate." She put her hand over her stomach and made a face. "Ugh. That cheeseburger is not setting well and Jack's steak sandwich smelled disgusting."

I raised an eyebrow as she went to go sit on the couch. "You all right?" I asked. "Not gonna spew, are you? Because I will be really pissed if you puke on my red shag rug." I had a brief recollection of saying basically the same thing to Chris and wondered why I spent so much time making sure my friends weren't going to urp.

"Nah, I'm fine. I just need to go to bed, I think."

"All right, sleep well... You sure you don't want a garbage can or something?"

She giggled. "I'm fine, Mickaela. Go to bed."

I frowned, feeling a sense of déjà vu. I headed to my bedroom and had just gotten comfortable under the covers and closed my eyes when I heard a gag noise followed by what sounded like running followed by more gagging noises. My eyes flew open. "Oh hell no!" I exclaimed, throwing the covers off and charging back into the kitchen. My vision tinged with red when I saw Roseanne hunched over my sink doing the very thing she said she wasn't going to do. "What the *hell*?" I cried.

"I'm so sorry," she muttered as she ran the sink water. "I'm so sorry."

"Oh my gosh, Roseanne, seriously?" I tangled my fingers in my hair as a flashback caused my temper to reach its boiling point. A flashback of my ex-husband puking all over both bathrooms and the entire hallway and clogging the sink once in a drunken stupor, all of which I had to take care of while he blindly bounced off of objects till he found the bed. "Dude, I had to clean up my ex's puke! Now I have to clean up yours too!"

"I didn't get it on your rug," she garbled right before she heaved again.

I stared at her, and my anger deflated as I watched her helplessly wretch into my kitchen sink.

"That cheeseburger...was not okay," she muttered.

I sighed and ran my hand across her back in a comforting gesture. "Good thing you didn't eat the steak sandwich."

She laughed in spite of the situation, and about an hour later after everything had been cleaned up, we finally went to sleep.

The offhanded comment about her moving in next door hadn't been something either one of us really took all that seriously at the time, but the idea stuck with Roseanne, and in January, the anniversary of my second year in my studio, she made the end apartment her home. By that time, Jack had been evicted for failure to clean up his hoarding mess on the driveway, I'd had a drug bust go down after I'd called the cops because I'd heard gunshots in the alleyway in the middle of the night during a thumping hip hop party in the apartment behind me, and I had gone completely out of my comfort zone and went on a random trip down to Huntington Beach to visit my bartender friend, which had resulted in igniting my long-forgotten sense of adventure and wanderlust.

I was beginning to embrace my singleness. I was starting to enjoy the freedom that came with it. I was no longer mourning the "what could have been" of my failed marriage because "what could have been" really was a "what was never going to be." Roseanne was in the exact same place in her life, so having her move next door just made sense. We'd be a force to be a reckoned with, independent women who could enjoy life just fine without the presence of a man.

It was the first time since moving in that I started to feel a sense of liberation, and with it came a great sense of contentment. Almost enough to drown out the lingering loneliness.

Chapter Four

Hailing Cabs and Bar Poetry

During March of 2011, there was this thing called the "supermoon" that was getting a lot of hype. Apparently, it is when the moon is closest to the earth, and this one was supposed to be bigger than normal, or some such who knows what. I didn't pay that much attention at the time. I should have, but I didn't.

While Roseanne and I were on this "single ladies are awesome" kick, we had been taking a road trip somewhere every year for about three years, starting right after I had left my ex-husband and not long after Roseanne had been cheated on by her longtime jerk of a boyfriend. Even though she had entertained the idea of a couple of guys since then, and one or two may have caught my attention in passing, we still held true to the road trip tradition, and this year was no different. This year, we were off to San Francisco, a favorite city of both of ours and one we couldn't wait to get back to.

March was an iffy month to travel in where we lived since we had to drive over a giant mountain pass to get to California, but we figured March was close enough to spring that we would be fine.

First two days were pretty all right. Rainy but manageable. We had gotten into San Francisco without much issue and had spent our time shopping and gossiping and generally doing what girls do best.

We ran into trouble the night we went to the ballet.

We'd decided to take a cab so we didn't have to worry about directions, and we went to a fancy Italian dinner in Little Italy. Afterwards, we went to the ballet, but the rain was nothing more than a dreary drizzle.

Fast forward three hours, and I was rushing through the

lobby of the opera house, trying to find Roseanne since I had gone to the bathroom and she had gone out to go smoke a cigarette. I finally braved going outside, even after seeing the horizontal rain flying by out the doors, and screamed as soon as I stepped foot out of the building. I tried to shield myself with my umbrella, but it almost instantly turned inside out.

I spotted Roseanne on the far side of the building, huddled next to some shrubs and talking to a random guy about lord knew what. I shlogged my way over to them, getting pelted by rain and generally feeling like I was stuck in a tropical storm. "Oh my gosh, Roseanne!" I cried. "What are you doing? I'm about to lose my mind!" I had always had bad anxiety, and being pummeled to death by blowing frozen rain was a sure way to get my hackles raised. "Seriously!"

She must have heard the desperate note in my voice because she grabbed hold of my arm and started hauling me toward the bus stop across the street. "All right, the guy said that there is a bus stop over here. And you know where we are going, right?"

I nodded numbly as I tried to huddle under her umbrella. Before we'd gone on the trip, I'd asked my grandmother if she had an extra umbrella we could use. Who would have known that the ugly-patterned umbrella from the sixties or seventies would have been the one to withstand gale force winds and hurricane rain?

As we ran across the street in our best theatre dress, which was nothing formidable against this freakish storm, I thought about where we were heading and checked the sign at the bust station to make sure it was for real. We needed to get to Geary Street. It was where our hotel was, as well as the bar I wanted to take Roseanne to.

During all of this, I had a flashback to our previous trip to San Francisco, when I had done extensive research to find a rock club I wanted to go to and hadn't been able to go because of an unfortunate incident with some lesbians that resulted in Roseanne having the worst panic attack ever. I was so *not* going to be denied a chance to go to another place I wanted to go to this time! I already knew where this place was, and all I had to do was make sure we got there. Roseanne was the type of person who got annoyed after so long and just shut down and wanted to go to bed. Not me. I was a warrior. And I was going to get to this bar if it freaking killed me. Supermoon be damned.

We joined the group of twenty or more ballet-goers all trying to take refuge in one another at the bus stop as the wind and rain continued to pelt us like some sort of freakish apocalypse movie. To everyone's annoyance, every time a gust blew freezing wetness our way, the six or so college girls all huddled together and screamed in the kind of high pitch only cheerleaders could comprehend. It set everyone's nerves on edge and did nothing to make the bus come any faster.

As I stood there, shivering, soaking, and glad that the shoes I had on were open-toed heels because I could at least drain the water out of them, Roseanne tapped on my shoulder to get my attention. I glanced back at her and she pointed to where a little old man of maybe seventy-five was hunkered down against the weather, no umbrella, hands in his pockets, and his jacket collar up as his only protection. He was enduring it all like a trooper as the water sluiced off of him. I glanced at the shrieking girls, appalled that they all had umbrellas and not one of them gave two craps about the freezing old man suffering in silence.

I pointed to Roseanne's umbrella then over to the man, miming to the best of my ability with the torrential whooshing wind and the screaming idiots. She understood me and positioned herself next to the old man, shielding him from the downpour with her stalwart seventies umbrella.

The man muttered his thanks and continued to stand in stoic silence. Roseanne and I exchanged a look and she shook her head as if in disbelief over the fact that the other mob of people there had been so negligent. It was a moment where I truly appreciated my friend. Roseanne had a tendency to be loud, brash, and offensive to about ninety percent of the population, but she had a heart of gold and she genuinely cared about people. It was one of the reasons why I loved her, because we were the same that way. Despite both of our claims to be jaded and cynical and hardened to the world, when it came to someone in need, our hearts always got the better of us. It was probably why we had remained friends all these years.

Roseanne had done about eight hundred things I did not agree with, and I'm sure I had done about the same amount in her eyes. We were vastly different. But in this area, we were the same. We helped people who needed it. We helped friends who probably didn't even deserve it. We gave second chances to people who *really* didn't deserve it. Our hearts spoke the same language, and I loved her for that. She was one of the only people who had ever understood and accepted me despite our differences.

When the bus finally showed up, we mobbed it like some kind of zombie hoard, and packed it to the point where it was probably above capacity because no one even came to get our money. We all just stood there like drowned rats, staring blankly in silence. I don't even know if Roseanne and I spoke to one another until we reached our stop, or for that matter, if anyone in the bus spoke at all. It seemed we were all in a unanimous state of shock.

When the bus finally let us off at Geary, I was dismayed to realize that 1—it was still raining just as hard, and 2—while we were on the right street, we were still probably about twelve blocks away from our destination. The stress was making my eyes hurt. I tried in vain to hail a cab, and about three of them sailed past me without a care in the world.

"We should just go back to our hotel," Roseanne muttered.

Oh no! I knew that exhausted tone in her voice. No way was I letting her bail on me again! It was time for drastic measures if I wanted to get to where I wanted to go. The stress and annoyance that was making my eyes bulge apparently morphed into some kind of crazy adrenaline because, suddenly, I had just freaking had it.

I spotted a cab about a block away, speeding our direction with no intention of stopping, and I jumped out into the middle of the street like a crazy person, waving my arms like I was flagging down an airplane. Needless to say, the cab stopped.

I yanked the door open and we piled in, grumbling to the driver where we were headed.

"Geez, Mickaela," Roseanne murmured. "You're insane."

"I just want a freaking beer," I griped. The ballet had been six kinds of boring, the nosebleed section we had been in had been so hot that I was nursing a migraine, which had not been helped by the screaming banshees at the bus top. I was soaked and about two seconds away from hypothermia. I was so over it. When I got it in my head that something was going to get done, it got done. Period.

When we reached our destination, finally, we argued briefly with the cabbie about the fare since the Einstein had forgotten to turn the meter on, and we ambled out. Luckily, the rain had stopped, but the place that I remembered being posh and chill was jammed with people and thumping bass from the DJ spinning 90s and Top 40 rap and hip hop. It put my teeth on edge and I headed toward the bar. I was severely in need of something alcoholic to calm my frazzled nerves.

I sent Roseanne out to scout for seats for us while I ordered a beer for me and some Jager for her. While waiting for the snail of a bartender, a tall, frizzy-haired man who looked like Fabio at sixty if he'd done drugs for twenty years swaggered over to me.

He leaned against the bar with an arrogant smirk and muttered a greeting.

I raised an eyebrow and did my best to be polite while simultaneously searching for how far along the bartender was in the progress of making our drinks. It was a beer and a shot. How hard could it be?

"This DJ is really good," he said, flipping his gray hair over his shoulder.

I stared. I couldn't help it. This was absurd. I looked past his shoulder for Roseanne and saw that she had snagged a seat close to the fireplace. I forced a smile and nodded at the man, hoping my lack of response would make him go away.

"You here alone?"

"Uh...no," I said forcefully. "My friend and I are on vacation."

If possible, his lecherous gaze got even creepier. Lucky for me, the bartender showed up at that moment with our drinks. I flung the money on the counter and strode away as swiftly as I could given the crowd of people. Creeper Fabio's eyes followed me over to Roseanne and me and I was bothered by it until a buxom brunette sauntered up to the bar and distracted him.

Whew. Dodged that bullet.

Although, I had to admit, getting hit on was nice, even though I only ever seemed to get hit on by weird people.

Roseanne downed her shot of Jager and had two more and a beer before she finally felt relaxed and ready to dance, which was amazing since Roseanne didn't dance. But, really, how could we not? Everyone was, and they were playing old school stuff from our high school years.

We chair danced for awhile, which is always easier—less limbs to worry about—and finally progressed to moving out onto the dance floor. My nerves had finally relaxed and we were laughing and being silly, what we usually did best. The two of us never had an issue making idiots out of ourselves.

Buzzed, Roseanne finally shouted over to me, "I'm really horny!"

I raised an eyebrow and shouted back, "Yeah, that makes two of us!" I hadn't had sex since I was married. I didn't believe in premarital sex. So, there was that. I was human, after all. If I was a guy, I'd have a permanent affliction with which blue was part of the title.

"But we're single!" she cried in despair.

And for some reason, that was hilarious. We giggled and high-fived one another like it was some kind of accomplishment. It was a true *Sex in the City* type moment.

We danced some more before Roseanne really did start to look like she was going to drop dead, and we hoofed it back to the hotel. Thankfully, it had stopped raining.

When we got there, however, I felt broody and restless, not yet ready to go to sleep. I glanced at the clock and, since it was still decently early, I told Roseanne I was going to go to the restaurant across the street and to go ahead and go to sleep. She did so and I headed over to Tommy's Joynt, a place that was embedded in my memories as much as my ex was. And, really, I think that was half the reason I wanted to go.

I had taken Roseanne there the night before because I knew she would like it, but I still felt like I had to confront the ghosts of my past by myself, and Tommy's Joynt had a lot of ghosts. People spend a lot of time fearing the ghosts that they think are real, the supernatural creatures from beyond, but to me, the real ghosts you should fear are the ones of your own making. The memories from another life that haunt you, that make it impossible for you to move forward or move back. I had been dealing with these kinds of ghosts since I'd moved into my studio. I had methodically eradicated a lot of them, but the ones from this place were some of the worst...because the memories were some of the best.

I went to the bar and ordered a Guinness, then sat at an empty table and pulled out a notebook I had brought with me. I felt like I was going to burst. I had too many indecipherable emotions swirling around inside of me and the only way to purge them was to write some kind of bizarre, obscure poetry. So I did.

I'm not really sure how long I sat in there. All I know is that no one bothered me, which I was grateful for, I got out some kind of depressing poem, I briefly contemplated how sad it was that I was sitting alone in a bar/restaurant writing poetry, and I came to a startling realization.

I was really tired of being alone.

As much as I had come to love my independence. As much as I loved these girl adventures with my BFF.

There was something missing.

Something I craved.

Part of my brain bounced back to my conversation with Chris, the conversation I had at the time been so desperate to avoid. I hadn't really thought about it up till then. I had still been too hurt, too raw from everything. Most people said that in order to get over a relationship that had gone south, you had to go out there and start dating again, much like the "get back on the horse when you fall off" analogy. But I wasn't like everyone. I felt too deeply. The scars had not just scratched the surface, they had gone all the way through. If it was possible to feel one's heart obliterated, that's what I had felt. I honestly hadn't thought I possessed one anymore. Not in a romantic capacity at any rate.

But I sat there, in the place I had gone with my ex so many times, and I remembered. I allowed myself to remember and I let those memories wash over me and through me with a bittersweet kind of recognition. I didn't run from them. What would be the point? What was done was done, and what would be would be. So I re-lived those things. Part of my heart smiled. Part of my heart cried. But for the first time in too long, I actually felt my heart again. And on the heels of that realization, came an epiphany.

I really wanted another relationship.

I was ready.

I wasn't broken anymore.

And this terrified me.

Chapter Five

Dinner...

"Hey, is there any reason you know of as to why Terry is running laps around the storage shed?"

I frowned and looked up from where I was sitting on my couch, trying to ignore the fluttery feeling in my chest at the thought of my impending dinner with Deaven. Roseanne was on the other side of my screen door, smoking a cigarette out on my front step. "Um, not that I can think of." Terry was the Vietnam vet who had since moved into Jack's old place.

He was also a bit of an oddball, as I think that was a requirement of all tenants who lived there. "He's running laps?"

"Yeah. I was out here smoking and the next thing I know, I see him doing sprints around the storage shed over here."

I raised an eyebrow. "He's probably drunk...or high." It was a well-known fact that Terry was a raging alcoholic and took off at around seven a.m. every morning to grab his liquid breakfast at the corner liquor store. He'd also made a practice out of coming to my door during all hours of the night asking to use my phone because of one crisis or another, looking stoned out of his mind. I didn't know all that went on over there at his place. I didn't want to know. The only thing that mattered was that he let Roseanne and I park on his driveway, and he liked us enough that he watched out for us, which was great since he would have been really creepy otherwise. "Maybe he's having a flashback," I added.

She nodded. "Yep, true enough. He probably thinks Charlie is after him."

I giggled.

"Hey, you know Nick is moving out?"

"Really?" Nick was the stoner neighbor who'd nonchalantly watched the power line smoking.

"Yeah, he came out and yelled at me the other morning, told me you and I were too loud and he could hear everything that we said because the walls were so thin. I'm sure he really loved that tangent I went on when I found out Brian was still married." She rolled her eyes and took another drag.

Brian had been a guy Roseanne had been seeing for awhile. Seemed nice enough in the beginning, although strangely secretive and preoccupied with having me around all the time. He also liked to show up to Roseanne's place early before she got home from work, and would come over and hang out at my place for a half an hour. Super bizarre and rather annoying. Come to find out he'd never really divorced his wife and had been taking Roseanne for a ride. It had not gone over well when she had found out.

"I'm sure he also enjoyed the fight we had in the middle of the night."

Roseanne laughed. "Yeah, we fight just like we talk. No one can get a word in edgewise and all we do is interrupt each other."

A month or so prior, Roseanne and I had gone out with my ex-husband to get a couple drinks. While I'd been in the bathroom, all hell had broken loose and I'd come out to the two of them screaming at one another outside of the bar. The same bar, coincidentally, where I had met Deaven. It had irritated me so badly, the two of them going at it like children, that I hadn't even bothered to find out what exactly was going on. I'd just turned and bailed, stomping home in the rain—barefoot no less. I couldn't stride angrily in heels. When Roseanne had gotten home, we'd duked it out verbally, which never happened with us. We didn't fight. Like ever. Roseanne was the emotional one, the volatile one. I was the rational, calm one. We balanced one another out. It was how our friendship worked.

But I am not made of stone, contrary to popular belief at that time. And I had a temper of my own. I may have had a longer fuse than her, but when I blew, it wasn't pretty. And neither one of us had actually "blown," so to speak. But we'd both been seriously aggravated, and we had spent the better part of an hour trying to out-shout one another in her apartment. When that had gotten us virtually nowhere, we had decided to discuss the situation like rational adults. Amazing how much better that works out.

All this time, my ex-husband had been holed up in my apartment because he had followed me home to make sure I didn't get kidnapped or mugged or something during my tromp of protest. I wasn't really happy with either of them, and by the time I'd finished patching things up with Roseanne, I just wanted to be alone to try and process the ridiculousness that had been my evening. My ex-husband telling me—not asking me, *telling* me—that he was going to crash on my couch for the night was the final straw.

I was very territorial about my apartment. It was *mine*. I had found it, I had made it my lair, it was my space, and I was selective about who I shared it with. While I didn't have an issue with him being there normally, I was annoyed, and I needed to decompress. It was impossible to decompress with my ex around. That was just ten kinds of weird I wasn't ready to even try and deal with.

So, I told him to take a hike. Guy had to walk home about two miles, but it wouldn't kill him. A small part of me felt bad, but the majority of me was still so full of animosity I didn't care. It was a strange line I tried to walk there for awhile with my ex-husband. While I did care about him and wanted to remain friends, I had so much resentment toward him that the two opposing ends warred with one another on a regular basis. In the end, I'd had to distance myself in order to regain my sanity and move on completely. I couldn't remain in some whacked-out limbo for the rest of my life, teetering between being an independent woman and my ex's go-to person.

It had worked out good for everyone in the end. I still talk to him. He's married now and doing his thing. He seems happy enough, playing his guitar and going to heavy metal shows. I've never wanted anything but the best for him.

But I'm getting off topic.

The point was, that had been the last time I'd gone out with my ex. The last time before the night he'd guilted me into going out with him again a month later, which had ironically been the same night I'd run into Deaven after ten years.

And now, I was sitting on my couch, pretending to be nonchalant and gossip with Roseanne when my insides were a mess and my heart felt like it was going to erupt from my chest.

"So, you're going out with Deaven again tonight?" she asked, rubbing out her cigarette butt on the concrete.

I swallowed as my heart stumbled over itself in anticipation. "Yeah." I sounded so much more casual than I felt.

She snorted. "Well, good luck with that. No matter how great he seems now, he's just going to end up a douchebag like all the others."

I stared at her for a moment, trying to register the fact that she would be such an intentional buzzkill when she knew how happy I had been the night before. I understood she was doubly bitter because of her last failed relationship, but did that mean she had to rain on my parade when I was— strangely—excited to be going out with a guy for the first time in longer than I could remember? I'd spent the last two years seconds away from being A. a crazy cat lady, or B. a Femi-Nazi. For reasons I didn't even want to dwell on for too long because it would scare the crap out of me if I did, none of those raging, angry, hostile feelings toward all things male had surfaced when I'd been talking with Deaven. No voice in the back of my head telling me what a waste of my time it was to even indulge him in conversation, or telling me to abort mission as soon as possible because I was venturing into a danger zone. All I'd felt was...happy.

Was it really so wrong that I wanted to hold onto that for a little while? My newfound liberation and contentment with being by myself had helped me to realize I needed to take my happy moments when I could get them. That life wasn't a picnic, but moments could be amazing if you allowed yourself to have them. So why should I slam the door on one that was staring me in the face? Maybe it would turn out to be nothing but a good time catching up with an old friend. So what? That was still a hundred times better than working myself into the grave like I did every other night of my life.

Annoyed, I stood up. "Yeah, well, I have to go get ready, so I'll talk to you later." I wasn't usually so dismissive, especially of Roseanne, but the lump that was forming in my stomach as the seconds ticked closer to my dinner date was demanding more of my attention, and I didn't want my evening to be dampened by doubts she had put in my mind. For once, I just wanted to experience something great instead of analyzing it to death and coming up with a list of reasons why it was a bad idea.

Somewhere in the back of my mind, I heard Chris laughing at me in triumph. Who would have thought that one set of gorgeous blue eyes and a smile that could light the world on fire would have suspicious me all addled? And it hadn't even taken much more than a conversation and a few subtle flirtations. Either this guy was something special, or I was really losing my man-eating edge.

I chose something casual to wear, a flowy, artsy black shirt and some jeans. Simple-classy with enough of a "blank canvas," so to speak, to rock out some great turquoise accessories. Plus, it was a black shirt, which meant it would hide the pit stains the size of Lake Ontario that I would no doubt be sporting during dinner. Hey, come on now. This is real life. And unlike the romance novels I edited, this heroine had a real life condition called hyper hydrosis, which in everyday language translated to—I was sweaty as heck. Like, all the time. Over the years, I'd figured out nifty tricks to hide this not so attractive betrayal of my genetic make up. So yeah, everyone thought I was a dreary goth because 80% of my wardrobe was black. Nope, just practical.

Okay, well...maybe I was a *little bit* dreary goth...

But mostly just practical.

So, on my way out the door, I debated on which shoes to wear. Regular nice, black old faithfuls, or sparkly, sassy shoes that were a size too big for me?

I decided on the sparkly ones. They would lend a "pop" of color to my otherwise monotonous outfit. Besides, it's not like I was going to be running a marathon. I was going to be sitting at a table. I was sure I could manage not to trip and fall on my face for the small jaunt across the room.

I chided myself for being as jittery as I was as I made my way to the restaurant. It was stupid to feel so nervous. He was a guy. Big deal. A guy I'd basically known as a kid. I'd always been one of the guys. This time should be no different than any other time I went out with an old friend.

I tried to rationalize myself into the dirt, but some part of me refused to believe my logic. Something felt different about Deaven. Something always had.

But regardless of how flustered I felt, I would never show it. I strode into the restaurant with purpose, and zeroed in on him sitting at a table in the back. My heart did some kind of gymnastics routine. Traitorous organ.

"Hey!" I greeted cheerfully, hoping I didn't look stressed, or overeager, or ridiculous, or...

Sit down and chillax. Stop being a spaz.

I did so, avoiding hugging him like I would normally do when I met up with someone. I didn't want to seem forward and like I thought this was a date. I was catching up with an old friend. That was all. Although, in the back of my mind, I wondered why I was thinking this scenario to death. Any other time I was "meeting up with an old friend," I was nonchalant and probably would have gone in jeans and a heavy metal t-shirt, not giving a crap what I looked like. I sure as heck wouldn't have worn sparkly freakin' shoes. None of this made any kind of normal sense to me and it was freaking me out already.

I sat down after exchanging the required pleasantries and stuffed my face into my menu to try and remember how to function like a human. I asked him about his job. That was a safe topic.

Surgical tech. Nice.

I listened to him talk about that while I perused the menu and ordered a glass of wine. I was in no way, shape, or form a slave to the grape, but when it came to needing to relax in a hurry, it was my failsafe. Sad? To some maybe. But when anxiety had been my constant companion for over a decade, a glass of vino was a much lesser evil than having a panic attack and scaring away any human being within a hundred feet of me.

I finally braved a real glance up at Deaven once my food was ordered and they took my menu from me. I chided myself—again—for feeling so ridiculous. At one time, I had been a social creature and somewhat of a tease....okay, a lot of a tease. I'd been flirtatious and fun and could draw in a lot of people with charisma I didn't even remember now. I looked back on that person like she was an alien.

Oh geez. What was wrong with me? What in the world had happened to me over the last ten years? I couldn't even blame it on my ex. I had done this to myself. My ex was who he was and had always been. He hadn't done anything other than be who he was. It was me who had reacted to life the way I had, who had done what I had to lock myself away in some kind of self-made prison to protect...what? Who? I didn't even know now. That person from forever ago felt as foreign to me as if I'd just randomly been introduced to a stranger on the street.

Some warped part of me wanted to just go home and go back to the yo-yo weird carousel that had been my relationship with my ex for however long. Because it was safe and this whole thing was scary as hell.

I'm not ready for this.

Yes, you are. You've known you were ready since that night in Tommy's Joynt last month.

What are you talking about? This isn't *a date! It's catching up with an old friend.*

Whatever you want to delude yourself with.

Please, are you really that *stupid?*

He doesn't think of it that way.

How do you know? Stop trying to shoot yourself in the foot.

Oh. My. Gosh. How many voices *were* there inside of my head? Good grief!

Instead of pondering this disturbing question, I asked Deaven about his trip to Europe he had mentioned when I had been talking to him the night before. That was an interesting topic that took up a decent amount of time, and since the furthest place I'd ever managed to venture was New York City when I was fifteen, I was hopelessly intrigued, if not more than a little envious.

When that thread had run dry, our food had come and I was markedly more relaxed because of the wine. So, I asked him about his failed marriage. That was what I really wanted to ask him in the first place. I wanted to know that I wasn't alone in that regard.

Plus...

Let's just face it. About four years prior while I was living out of state and randomly social network-stalking pretty much everyone I knew out of boredom, I had run across Deaven's ex-wife's page. I wouldn't have known they were married if her profile picture hadn't been the two of them, but I remember thinking, *Oh good lord, he didn't marry* that *chick! Not Deaven!* Because I'd apparently always had some sort of weird thing for Deaven, and I hadn't liked that girl since she'd tried to steal my boyfriend in a thrift store at age sixteen.

Anyway...

He told me the brief story, ending with that she had cheated on him. I felt sad for him. No one with that beautiful of a smile, blue eyes like that, and the creative streak he had shown me should end up being cheated on.

Gimme a break. You know nothing about him. Superficial much?

That's not true. I know he holds a good conversation, he loves the written word like I do, and he is fun. I remembered that from so long ago...

How was it that I had a better conversation with him in our teenage years than I had had probably since then?

"So, what about you?" he asked me.

I stared for a second, then launched into what I always said. "Well, I was married for awhile, but I'm divorced now. My ex-husband, he's a good guy, but he had some things he needed to sort out, that he still needs to sort out—"

Deaven interrupted me with a shake of his head. "I have things I need to sort out too. We all have things we need to sort out."

I blinked, taken aback by his rebuttal. "Well, we are still on good terms and everything," I blurted, feeling strangely protective of my ex. After all, he *was* a good guy, if somewhat misguided. I'd always been his champion. I had a super hero complex. I really did. I saw people's potential and latched onto it, believing in them more than they believed in themselves. Sometimes that worked and really helped somebody. Other times, it only ended up being toxic to me. I hadn't figured out how to tell the difference at the onset of the relationship yet, and by the time I realized I was in something unhealthy, I was more than likely already drained of my life force.

But before I could really think more on this subject, I had already launched into my litany of reasons why my ex was the way he was. Deaven listened to me patiently and with a piercing blue-eyed intensity that I usually would have found unnerving, but for some reason, with him, I just found it sexy. When I had exhausted my speech, one of those voices in my

head whispered, *Why are you talking so much about your ex?*
I blinked. Did I always do that? I did. When had my life become so entwined with his that I no longer knew how to talk
about myself and instead spent all my time defending him?

I would be lucky if Deaven even finished dinner with me
after that novel of ex-husband-defense that had just purged
itself out of my mouth. Ready for a relationship? Sure. Maybe
when I opened my door one morning and found a leprechaun
there in a little green suit telling me his rainbow had managed
to land there and he had a pot of gold with my name on it.

"You know," he finally said after I sat there quietly con-
templating what was wrong with my head. "I don't know the
guy, so I can only speak from personal experience here. I'm
sure he has all of those problems that you just told me
about, but a lot of people have problems. *I* have problems. I
deal with depression, my childhood wasn't the greatest; in
fact, I grew up in circumstances similar to what you just de-
scribed your ex went through. I had a marriage based entirely off of lies. Things happen that really suck, and we don't
always have control over them, but you have a choice as to
how you handle those things. You can spend your life blam-
ing everything on everyone else and feeling sorry for yourself, or you can choose to do something else with your life."
He shrugged his broad shoulders in a manner that was so
much more nonchalant than the potent words he was wield-
ing my direction. "I choose to not let the things that happen
to me in my life dictate who I am. There is no sense in whin-
ing and crying about what happens or has happened. It
doesn't change anything. I feel like the things I've been
through have taught me something, and I try to use that to
make myself a better person."

I stared at him for a few seconds before nodding.
"Yeah...you're absolutely right." And he was. But it was so
much more than that. He had literally just summed up pretty
much everything I tried to live my life by. I was dumbfound-
ed by the fact that someone else actually took that way of
life to heart, but what really got to me was the fact that I
suddenly saw over half the human relationships I had were
with people who would rather play the victim than fight to be
better, who would rather complain and say "poor me" than
do something to change their lives. Why? Because I thought

I could help them. Forget that, all I was doing was enabling them.

How come I hadn't seen that before?

How had his words caused illumination when I had been ambling along, blindly playing therapist for who knew how long?

"So, I know we've been going on and sharing about our past relationships," he said suddenly. "I'm wondering, are you looking for a relationship right now?"

I arched my eyebrows, surprised at his blunt question, but happy with the fact that he wasn't afraid to just get to the point. "Um...yeah, maybe...I'm not really sure." *Smooth delivery, Mickealea.* I glanced at my almost finished food and drained the last of my wine glass. "Why?"

"Well, I can tell there is a decent amount of chemistry between us."

He could? Oh good. Apparently, I was still able to flirt like a normal human being. That was encouraging information.

"I just...I'm not sure if I want anything serious right now, or a relationship at all, actually."

The weird part of my heart that kept getting all fluttery and doing stupid crap felt like it fell into my feet, which was ridiculous, but it happened all the same. And the idiot voices came back.

You're stupid for thinking he would like you, Mickaela. No one can like you, let alone love you.

You weren't good enough for your marriage. That failed in an epic manner. What makes you think you would be good enough for even one second of this man's attention?

Who is he? No one. Just a guy. Why do you care so much?

Because he's a guy who is beautiful. I know it. I can feel it. You're a freaking idiot.

I felt tears sting my eyes and I messed with my napkin, twisting it and tearing off shreds. "So then, what?" I spat, unable to keep the contempt out of my voice. "You just brought me here to waste my time?"

He looked slightly taken aback by my venomous response.

"No, I just—"

Go home, Mickaela. Flee while you can. Just get the heck

out of there before this hurts even worse.
Why does it hurt so much anyway? This wasn't even a
date.
It hurts because I am stupid.
"Look, I really like you. We have really good conversation and you don't mind my sick sense of humor." He tried to make light of it and reached across the table to touch my hand. I immediately yanked it away, feeling all kinds of jumbled and messed up. "I still want us to be friends. I just don't know what I want right now in terms of anything more than that. From you or anyone. I just thought I'd get that out of the way, lay all my cards on the table."

Some small sliver of sense returned to me and I understood what he was saying. It wasn't so different from where I had been in my life only last year, or even up until a month prior. I attempted to blink back the tears that were pending, and one succeeded in escaping anyway. Awesome. What a basket case I was.

"Oh great, I made you cry the first time I went out with you," Deaven said, flashing me a teasing smirk.

I rolled my eyes and waved my hand. "Yeah, well...sorry, I really thought you were just telling me to get lost for a minute there." I shook my head. "I guess I'm used to having people just decide I'm not worth their time and I really enjoy your company so it sucked thinking you didn't want anything to do with me."

"No, that's not what I meant at all. I enjoy your company too. I'd like for us to still hang out. I just wanted to be honest and up front with you so we could make sure we were on the same page and you didn't think I was leading you on."

I gave him a small smile. "It's fine, I appreciate your honesty. It's refreshing." And that was the truth. The voices quieted, appeased with the knowledge that he did in fact want to be friends with me. For some reason that was just as obscure as everything else I had felt thus far, that seemed really important to me. I didn't know what my deal was with Deaven. I didn't even want to try and linger long enough to analyze it. For some reason, even when I'd been eighteen, something had just felt right with him. Maybe it was just that he was the kind of friend who could really get me. That was fine. I could totally live with that. I just knew the thought of him vanishing again after all this time felt wrong. I wanted to know him. *Really* know him. In whatever capacity he could give me. It was so not the rational way I tried to face my life, but it felt right. Somewhere inside of me, it made sense.

And I was going to go with it.

As if sensing that his grin was my kryptonite, he turned its full power on me suddenly. "Hey," he said, "how about we get out of here and go get a drink?"

He could have asked me to go to the moon and I would have. Maybe it was because I felt he really listened to me. Maybe it was because he was someone from before everything I felt had messed me up. Maybe it was because he had charisma oozing out of him like freaking radiation. I wasn't going to sit there and question it. It was the same as when I'd met him as a teenager.

He was fun. Period.

I felt like I could be myself with him. Period.

Even as weird and jacked as that self was. He still wanted to hang out with me. Even after my small freak out moment. That was saying something.

I smiled at him. "Of course I do."

Chapter Six

...And Breakfast

"Holy crap, it's freezing out here!"

I giggled as Deaven and I made our way back to his car, and in not my first moment of boldness of the night, I reached over and put my arm around his shoulders playfully. He had no jacket on, I did, and any excuse to touch him at this point was well worth it. We had spent the last several hours having the best conversation of my life, and I was not going to relinquish any enjoyment this night produced because of me over-analyzing, second-guessing myself, or wondering what he wanted out of the situation.

Screw it.

He was an up-front kind of guy. He had already "laid his cards on the table," so to speak. There was noting wrong with flirting, and so long as he was going to let me do it, I was going to. It felt good to flirt and play again, and it felt even better to have it reciprocated. Because who cared about what he said about wanting a relationship? He was obviously okay with flirting, and that was more than okay with me. It was more fun than I'd had in ages.

It was humorous to me to walk back to where he had parked his car because it really *was* freezing, being early spring in the mountains. He was about three inches shorter than me, which didn't bother me, but made me feel like some sort of Amazonian lumbering colossus as we trekked back to his car with my arm around his shoulders like I was the dude. What was great was the fact that he was fine with it. I didn't threaten his manhood in some bizarre way. He just took everything in stride with that smile that would be the death of me.

"So, I have a bottle of wine back at my place," he informed me when we reached his car. "Would you like to come over for awhile?"

Like he needs to ask me that *question.* "Sure," I said, sounding so much more casual than I felt. Truth was, I didn't want this night to ever end, and the longer he wanted to be around me, the happier I was. I laughed more when I was with Deaven. Much more. And I spent more time not dwelling on what the "shoulds" and "should nots" of a situation were. I found that when I was with him, I felt free. Everything just was what it was, and that was amazing. I spent so much time trying to be in control of everything—my jobs, my finances, my emotions. It was freakin' exhausting. Deaven made all of that staunch rigidness vanish.

He drove me back to where I had parked my car, and I followed him back to his place, which was actually just his uncle's basement, but I didn't care. The guy was a self-proclaimed gypsy. His living space meant nothing to me. After all, I was living in a studio apartment that wasn't much bigger. Like I could be one to judge.

I attempted to seat myself on his couch in a dignified manner, even though my shoes were giving me issues because they were too big and trying to fall off, and he poured me a glass of wine.

"I bought this bottle earlier," he informed me. "Over at the place where we met. I went in there and asked them what a good red wine was." He shook his head as he finished pouring his glass. "Don't even ask me what this cost, because I am not going to tell you."

I laughed, touched that he had gone out of his way to buy a bottle of wine to share with me. I took a sip and raised my eyebrow and my glass. "Well, you picked well."

He took a sip and sat on the couch opposite me. "I did, didn't I?"

I laughed again and shuffled around on the couch, trying to get comfortable. "These shoes are ridiculous," I muttered, more to myself than anyone else.

"Dude, why don't you just take them off?" he queried.

I glanced up at him and debated for a half of a second before I just admitted, "I have hyper hydrosis. If I take my shoes off, I'm gonna slime your couch."

"I don't care if you sweat on my couch," he stated.

Really? There was a first. Most everyone I met thought my overactive sweat glands were nasty. One point for not caring, and two points for knowing what hyper hydrosis actually was. I took my shoes off.

He smiled and my heart melted, and before I knew what was going on, he asked me if he could share some of his poetry with me. Like I would ever say no. Hot man who I was seriously jonesing for reading me his creative work? That was like foreplay to a literary geek like me.

The first several things he shared, his voice wavered slightly with nerves, and he fidgeted, but the more he shared—and the more wine we drank—he became more relaxed and open, sharing personal things that all but brought me to tears.

And finally, he sat down next to me and said, "I wrote this one just last night. It's about the women who have touched my life, good or bad. You're in it." At my undoubtedly surprised expression, he shrugged and said, "What can I say? We have really good conversation. And I feel like you appreciate me. I don't know. You get where I'm coming from as far as writing is concerned, and that can only be a boon to one's craft, so I figure that's a good thing."

Would it have been weird from anybody else? Maybe.

Was it from him? Not at all.

Anything that should have felt weird with Deaven felt anything but.

I listened to his poem of girls past and present, ending with me and a strange, convoluted mix of emotions that pretty much reflected how I felt. It made me cry.

It made me cry because it validated what I felt. I wasn't a crazy person. I wasn't desperate. Deaven and I had something magnetic, something special. And it didn't even matter what it was. It didn't need a label. It was just special. And whatever that was, was awesome. I decided then and there, as I wrapped my arms around him and sniffled, that I wasn't going to question it. He had already brought more beauty and acceptance to my life than I thought I deserved. I was so over rejecting beautiful things that came my way. Forget it. If this man could bring some kind of light back to my dreary existence, I was gonna let him.

It was my mother text messaging me that brought me back to reality.

Are you still at Deaven's? was the question.

I glanced at the time.

Holy crap! It was 5:45 a.m! How had we managed to go through the entire night and into the morning without even realizing it? I shot my mom back a quick text. *Yes, I am at Deaven's. I am just leaving. I am completely irresponsible. Love you.*

I knew she would laugh because I was *always* responsible. She would know I'd had an amazing time. I would never stay out so late otherwise. "Oh my goodness," I muttered to Deaven. "It is almost dawn, I have to go!" I had never lost a whole night to incredible conversation before. Not ever.

I gathered my things and stuffed my sparkly shoes back on my feet.

"Hey, do you have anything you need to do today?"

I glanced up at Deaven and thought about the sixteen tons of editing I needed to get done. "No," I lied. "Nothing really." Aw man, the next couple days were gonna suck.

"Well, if you want, you can come back over later today and we can listen to some music. My uncle's out of town and we can listen to his system."

I had half an idea of what that meant, but I didn't care how much I understood. More time spent with Deaven meant more time smiling, and I suddenly found myself craving it—both the smiling and his company—more than I ever imagined I could crave anything. "Yeah, okay," I said with a grin as I slung my bag over my shoulder and headed for his door. "I had a really great time tonight," I said as I turned back to him.

"So did I," he answered.

He hugged me, and I had something weird click inside of my brain. All of those voices from before seemed to vanish, and all I heard was the one that was the loudest saying, *Don't think about it. Don't question it. Listen to your gut. What will be will be.* And that calmed any raging, tempestuous thought I might have had otherwise. At that moment, I had that moment, and *that moment* was insanely awesome. That was good enough for me. It was completely unlike the armor-wearing, cynical, skeptical recluse I had turned into upon my divorce, but it held a strange glimmer of a person I barely recognized from long ago. A person I thought had been murdered by my sense of self-preservation. I was willing to see how many more remnants of that person I could discover.

I opened up his door and ascended the staircase from the basement. I was taken aback by the fact that it was already light outside and the birds were singing. I giggled to myself and turned back to Deaven. "Oh my gosh, it's dawn," I stated.

He laughed, and I cherished the sound in my very soul. "See you later?" he questioned.

I nodded. "Yeah, I'll text you when I get up." I made my way to my car, and as I walked up the pathway to my stalwart apartment, I grinned wider than I ever had. I glanced at Roseanne's apartment, hoping that, since it was a weekend, she was still asleep. I didn't want to have to explain anything or give a blow-by-blow. I just wanted to absorb everything.

And I did so, as I collapsed into bed with the biggest idiot grin on my face.

I was happier than I had been in longer than I could remember. I had just spent all night with a man who had shared actual conversation with me for all those hours without awkward pausing or looking at me like I'd grown a second head. He had bantered with me, teased me, validated me, shared his inner self with me, and invited me back for more.

And as I closed my eyes to the sounds of the birds singing and the rays of light filtering through my blinds, I thought to myself that *I* was the lucky one. Because anyone who was able to catch a glimpse into Deaven's radiant soul was lucky, but the person he *invited back*...well, that person...that person was me, wasn't it?

I fell asleep with that same stupid smile on my face.

Aaaand....now the awkward feeling was back. Awesome. Who would have thought that eight hours would cause all my anxiety to come rushing back?

Four hours of fitful sleep was all I'd had, because I kept replaying everything that had happened. And of course I'd had to go to Mom's and tell her everything, because that was what I did. Somehow, the day had flown by much faster than anticipated, and I was strangely 1—not hungover, and 2—much less tired than I usually was on only four hours of sleep. Had to be endorphins. It was the only explanation. That was cool, though, since I don't think I'd experienced the effect of those pesky things since I had been seventeen.

So, I had just spent, like, twelve hours with the man. You would think I would be okay with him at this point. But as he was making me a sandwich, I stood with both my arms crossed over my chest and my legs crossed over at the ankles, screaming, "don't approach me!" in the best way body language could manage, and having difficulty holding a conversation. Whhhhhyyyy? I had been babbling my ever-loving head off the night before. Why was I suddenly so quiet? Ugh, I hated my developed social anxiety.

So, I stuffed my face with my sandwich in order to avoid feeling weird about not talking, and when we had both finished, he took me downstairs to where his audiophile uncle had created a state of the art sound system.

"Here, you sit in this chair. It sounds good here," he instructed, and I did as I was told, taking the middle of three chairs lined up in a row in front of a monstrous sound system and amidst about a billion—and I am not exaggerating—CDs and vinyls. I tried to crack my shoulder, which really hurt, and Deaven questioned me about it.

"Oh, my shoulder gets really messed up from editing," I told him. "The way I have to sit in my chair, I get this terrible knot under my shoulder blade and it makes my left arm tingle and go numb." Truth was, it had been numb off and on for...about a year, I guess. Sometimes it hurt more than others, but the longer I spent sitting in front of my computer, the worse it was.

"I'll give you a massage while we listen if you want," he offered.

Sure! It was a really good excuse to have him touch me! Plus, I would never turn down a free massage. "Yeah, all right," I said, trying to sound nonchalant. In the back of my mind, I seriously felt like I had as a high school senior when I'd been teasing the drama department guys into making out with me. "Thanks."

He loaded up the CD player with an artist he wanted to share with me and turned out the lights. That confused me at first since I didn't think music needed to be listened to in the dark, but over the course of the evening, I began to understand that the less distractions there were, the more I paid attention to the sound and the lyrics of what I was listening to. My world became filled with the song and I existed in the here and now, not in the many random things that filled my head at any given moment in time.

And somewhere in between the change from CD to vinyl and from my Nightwish CDs to Metallica and Aerosmith, Deaven started rubbing the knots in my shoulder. I relished the kneading of my muscles because they hurt, and randomly, I felt the heel of his hand dig underneath my shoulder blade and felt a crunch-pop that suddenly brought blood and feeling rushing back into my left arm.

"Oh my gosh!" I cried, flexing my arm. "Holy crap, you fixed it! Dude, that has been hurting and numb for...I don't even know how long!" I was genuinely amazed.

"I could tell it was out. It just felt like it was ready, so I pushed it back in place," he replied. Looking back now, that was an oddly metaphoric thing to say. And while I know he was just talking about my literal shoulder, I can't help but draw a parallel to where I was emotionally at that point in my life. I was ready to move on, ready to turn the page...I just needed a push.

"Oh my goodness, you are amazing," I gushed. I couldn't help it. The shoulder thing was a big deal.

He chuckled and I settled back into my chair to enjoy the music. My heart jolted up into my throat and I almost choked on it when I suddenly felt Deaven's arms snake around my shoulders in a loose hold. He rested his chin on my shoulder and I just sat there while my heart attempted to leap out of my chest cavity. I blindly reached up to place my hands on his forearm, and I closed my eyes at the feeling of being held. I could barely recall the last time I had been held by someone.

I felt his nose in my hair, which I had sprayed into submission with loose curls. "Your hair smells so good," he murmured to me, so much more potent in the darkness with his breath whispering across my neck. "You smell like pomegranates."

The feel of his words caressing the sensitive skin just under my ear sent my nerves into ecstatic spasms. Yeah, so I was going to use that hairspray *all the time.* As hairspray *and* perfume, if need be.

I sighed and relaxed, any awkwardness I had felt earlier vanishing with his touch. His arms tightened around me, and I let the music take me away, along with the feeling of being close to Deaven.

And the realization crashed like a lightning bolt inside of my brain.

With Deaven was the *only* place I ever wanted to be.

Chapter Seven

Hillbilly Teeth and Time Travel

Inviting Deaven to my apartment was a big deal. I didn't even want to do it for awhile because I had this weird boundary thing in my head, and anyone who I didn't know well—especially after the one freak "friend" I'd had for awhile who really just wanted in my pants and who was, in fact, a complete stoner alcoholic who yelled at me in front of a crowd full of people and who Roseanne had told what-for to—was not allowed into my "sanctuary," otherwise known as my studio apartment. But I knew Deaven, right? Since...like, childhood, right?

It was as crazy as everything else thus far, but I wanted him in my place.

Still, though, I needed to get to know him a little more outside of the intimate setting of my apartment. And shut up, it *was* an intimate setting to me at the time. It was *mine.*

So, we had a couple of times where we met and had a meal. And during one of those meals, I noticed my tooth felt funny, but didn't think much of it.

My front tooth—FYI—was half fake because of an incident I'd had years earlier involving me being my friend's bridesmaid, and drinking a *whole helluva lot* of wine and champagne. Let's just say my front tooth and my knee cap became intimately acquainted. That's all that needs to be said about *that* incident.

Anyway, so Deaven and I had dinner, and I was stoked about the next day because he had invited me rock climbing...which...lord knows I knew nothing about and I was half tempted to blow off because it sounded about as interesting as watching golf, but then after that, he was coming over to my place for a wine and dinner pairing I had put together for him and my mom. Because my mom is my bestie and needed to meet the man I'd been going on and on...and on about.

The night after Deaven and I had dinner, I went home on Cloud 9, because that was where I spent most of my time after I'd been with Deaven, and I started my nightly routine of washing my face etc. While I was flossing, I noticed something weird, and to my horror, in the bathroom mirror, I watched as my half-fake tooth front came off with the floss and flopped into the sink.

I stared.

In eye-twitching panic.

And I immediately picked my porcelain filling up and shoved it back on to avoid the snaggle-toothed, hillbilly visage staring back at me.

My heart was pounding.

And, all right, this may seem ridiculous to anyone else, but I had been having a recurring nightmare for over half of my life involving my teeth falling out. So, you can imagine the effect of 1—losing half my front tooth in the first place, and 2—watching it fall out while I flossed.

Not to mention, the only thing I could see in my mind was Deaven's perfect grin, and I kept envisioning walking into the rock climbing gym the next day looking like I came straight outta the backwoods of the Appalachians. "Nishe to meet you," I'd whistle as I met Deaven's friends while a piece of my flying spit landed on someone's shoulder.

I briefly considered super gluing my filling back in, but then discarded that idea for fear I'd never get it off again and would damage my tooth even more than my knee already had five years prior.

With a groan, and tears welling in my eyes, I popped my filling back out and flung it in the trash. I snatched my phone and did the only thing I could think of at the time—I called my mom.

"Oh my gosh, my freaking tooth just fell out! I'm gonna look like a hick when I go climbing with Deaven tomorrow!"

And that was pretty much how that entire conversation went. After my mom had tried to calm me to the best of her ability, I searched through the phone book and left messages for every dentist I could find that I thought might do a rush job on me the next day. In the middle of this, my mom called me back and gave me the number of my cousin's dentist, who I also left a message with. Out of so many, *somebody* should take pity on me, right? I mean, all I needed was someone to stuff some composite on there. It wasn't like I needed a root canal.

After I had done everything I possibly could with it being ten o'clock at night, I picked my phone back up and dialed Deaven. I really needed to hear his voice, and find out if he was going to laugh at me in a relentless manner. I wouldn't blame him if he did. One of my oldest friends had when I told him what had happened. With the gut-busting *BWAHAHAHA!* that only someone who has known you since you were twelve can actually get away with.

"What's up?" Deaven asked when he picked up the phone.

I briefly relayed the evening's events to him and ended with a sigh and a muttered, "Thish ish a nightmare." All S sounds accompanied with a whistle. Wonderful.

His chuckle was soft and not mocking. "Well, if you can't get a dentist to take you tomorrow before we go climbing, don't stress about it. It's not like it's something you can help."

"Like I want to meet your friendsh looking like a hillbilly!" I cried.

"None of my friends are going to judge you, I promise. Just explain the situation, laugh about it, it'll be fine."

"It ish sho not fine," I mumbled. "That would be sho embarrashing. I do not want you to shee me like thish."

He chuckled again. "It's not that big of a deal. If anything, you will probably make me feel even more comfortable than you already do. I spent most of my childhood living in a trailer, so you looking like a hillbilly will just make me feel at home."

I laughed in spite of myself, and warmth flooded my chest at his playful teasing. I appreciated him making light of something he knew was disturbing to me.

"Seriously, don't stress. It'll be fine."

I got off the phone with him, happy that he had taken everything so in stride and had made me laugh, but still horrified at the thought of him seeing me with half a tooth. As I went to sleep, I just hoped with all my might that one of the dentists could fit me in the next day.

And thank goodness, one of them did. My cousin's actually. Sure, I had to drive out to the North Forty of nowehere-land to get to his office, but I didn't care. He'd squeezed me in at eleven o'clock and rock climbing was at one, so that was way beyond amazing to me. I would have driven across the state.

So, before heading to the dentist, I dressed in my cutest workout clothes—a black tank and some black and green Ca-pri stretch pants, which I had bought the week before with the specific purpose of wearing them climbing—and put full makeup on, knowing I was going to be heading to the rock gym right after my appointment. Normally, putting makeup on to go to the gym would be the stupidest thing ever and pointless to me, but it was Deaven. Case closed.

The one thing I did notice, however, as I got up to turn my paperwork in to the receptionist, was that the pants were a lot looser than they had been when I'd bought them. I had to keep pulling them up and I realized I had been bloated for obvious feminine reasons while trying said pants on original-ly. That figured. Oh well. They should be fine. It was annoy-ing, but they were cute and at least they weren't too tight and showing off any fat roll I may have had. I was decently in shape, but nowhere near the "no body fat" end of the spectrum. I had hips and butt for days and while my waist was small and I didn't have too much of a tummy, I was a little soft in places that used to not be. Any article of clothing that made me look skinnier was fine by me.

Although, I have to admit, I did become a tad bit con-cerned when the receptionist called me into the exam room and I had to hike my pants up to sit in the chair without them falling down. It seemed the longer I wore them, the looser they got.

"So, what do we have going on here?" the dentist asked when he came in to check me out.

I explained to the best of my ability without making my-self sound like I had been a drunk lunatic five years before. "It's not that big of a deal," I ended the conversation with. "I just need you to put this filling back in."

He glanced at the chart. "The message said this was an emergency?" He sounded more confused than upset.

"Yeah, a cosmetic emergency," I stated.

Well, it *was*.

"Yeah, that's what I was told. What's going on? You said you had an event you had to go to tonight."

"I'm having a dinner party," I replied. It wasn't a lie. He didn't need to know my "dinner party" consisted of two people.

For some reason, he kept asking me questions. What kind of dinner party? What was it for? Seriously, your hands are in my mouth. Stop talking to me.

"I have a date!" I finally exclaimed, which was apparently hilarious. With as much of a sigh as I could muster with two people poking around in my mouth and sucking my tongue up into the spit-sucker, I waited out the rest of the procedure, then thanked the dentist profusely when he showed me my non-snaggle-toothed reflection. In all reality, it was even better than the original job.

I paid my enormous, overpriced bill and headed out as quickly as I could to the rock gym, with Deaven texting me asking if I was going to be late. I showed up right on time and jumped out of my car to see him standing by the entrance.

"Show me your smile!" he yelled by way of greeting.

I was more than happy to.

He chuckled and gave me a hug, then ushered me inside where he proceeded to show me a lot of things that sounded like a foreign language. He taught me how to "belay" his friend Hayley, which was basically how to keep my climbing partner from falling to his or her death. No big deal. Sheesh. My grip was so tight on that rope I'm surprised I didn't pull something.

When it finally came time for me to climb myself, I looked up at the route I was supposed to take and thought to myself, *Dude, why is this a big deal? I'm climbing up a wall with a bunch of hand and foot holds. This looks like the easiest thing on the planet. Why is this entertaining?*

But I didn't voice my thoughts. Apparently, Deaven thought this was great, so why not give it a go?

I guess he had started me on the easy route, but at least it wasn't the kiddie route. That would have been really humiliating, since my mind was refusing to grasp the complexity of this activity because it looked so stinking simple. So, I strapped into my harness and got myself tied in and ambled on up the rock wall, tackling it like I did everything—with no forethought whatsoever. I made it to the top with little issue and then repelled back down like some kind of super hero. Deaven was excited about this. Apparently, he had been climbing with a lot of girls who didn't even complete the easy route. Seriously? Like...why? Wasn't that the point? Why even try if you were going to give up and not make it to the top? Wasn't the point to get to the top?

Sometimes, my logic is extremely basic, and this was one of those times. Later, much later, after I'd wimped out on several routes that were way beyond my skill level, I realized why people stopped mid-route. It was because they were so stinking exhausted with shaking muscles and sweat pouring out of every orifice that there was no possible way they could continue. But I'm talking pretty advanced routes at this point. The fact that other girls had wussed out on a basic route still boggles my mind to this day, especially since unless my muscles are literally liquefied from exertion, I don't know how to quit. I'm a little bit like a dude like that.

But that day, me making it to the top of an easy route was a big deal to Deaven, which was cool.

During the second route, which was a tiny bit more difficult, I did the same thing I did on the first one—I hulked my way up it with about as much finesse as a buffalo tap dancing.

I did, however, make it to the top...because at this point, I still had some weird mentality leftover from growing up with guys and thought that if I didn't make it to the end game, I was a loser.

I repelled back down, and Deaven immediately said to me, "Hey, nice thong."

My heart did a weird flop-thump and I turned around to look at my ass over my shoulder. Sure enough, my "cute" workout pants had dropped to three-quarters-of-a-cheek level. I hadn't noticed because of the harness I was wearing. "Oh geez," I muttered, grabbing my loosely-flapping waistband and hiking it up. I glanced around the gym. "Did anyone else see?" I was remarkably unperturbed by the fact that Deaven had just seen the full moon out in broad daylight. I was more concerned at the fact that some random stranger had seen it.

"Only Hayley," he replied.

"Oh...okay." Hayley didn't seem scarred for life and we all had the same parts, so no worries. Maybe I should have been more modest, but I had grown up with guys, had been somewhat of a childhood exhibitionist before that, and had been a theatre diva for the four years I was in high school. Body parts were body parts. Not like I could take it back now, so I may as well own it.

We spent the remainder of our afternoon doing random routes, and I found that, to my surprise, I actually really enjoyed climbing. It was more challenging than it looked and it was a way to work out without feeling like I was working out. Plus, Deaven said he needed a climbing partner, and I would be stupid if I turned away that opportunity to spend time with him. The man said he didn't want a relationship. Okay, fine. Being climbing partners wasn't a relationship...right? Insert evil smiley face here.

Later that night, my lats and all the muscles in my arms were screaming at me in ways I cannot even describe as I cooked dinner for Mom and Deaven. It was the first moment when I said to myself, *Wow, climbing might actually be a really good workout.* Little did I know how hooked to the sport I would become.

Dinner was ricotta stuffed chicken with roasted red pepper sauce paired with Cabernet Sauvignon. Mom had made some goat cheese bruschetta paired with a Sauvignon Blanc that Deaven had brought, and dessert was peach sorbet that went well with Moscato. It was the first "event" I had hosted since I'd been married before, and...actually...well, maybe the first event ever aside from one family dinner.

As a child, I had been enamored with my friend's mom. She had been a theatre person and an artist, and she had hosted many parties with which she would flounce around in artsy attire—skirts and flowy tops and black and the sort— always holding her glass of red wine. I had thought she was so classy, so refined, and I had told myself at the young age of thirteen that one day I would be doing the same. That I would have achieved that kind of success in life to host grand parties and drink wine. Because, at thirteen, you don't realize that you can host any kind of party you want and can be poor as a gutter rat and still manage to get a few bottles of Two-Buck-Chuck.

So, maybe my home was a ramshackle studio and we were drinking mid-grade to low-end wine. It was a really big deal to me. Luckily, my company did not seem to mind.

We chatted and laughed while we sampled the cuisine and tried to decipher the flavors the different wines brought out. After awhile, we all had a nice, happy buzz going, and I managed to find a CD of random songs from my childhood I had made for my mom years prior.

And that was how Mom and I wound up half-drunk in my kitchen singing show tunes at the top of our lungs. We were aware of Deaven, but oblivious to him all at the same time. Regardless, he seemed to get a kick out of being our one-man audience.

When the CD ended, Mom realized how late it was getting, and after me sitting down on the couch and the last song ending, Deaven had cuddled up against me like he was trying to attach himself. I didn't mind, of course, but Mom seemed undeniably uncomfortable. Not because she thought it was wrong, but more because she didn't want to seem like an interloper.

So, she headed for home and Deaven and I opted to watch some crazy movie about time travel.

The movie led to conversation, which Deaven and I shared a lot of, and before I knew it, we were talking more about our past relationships. I was surprised to find out that Deaven had been engaged not too long ago, but that she had backed out after half the wedding had already been planned.

"It was probably a good thing," he said. "I think one of the main reasons I was attracted to her was because I thought she was safe. I figured she would be the person least likely to hurt me." He snorted. "My judgment was off on that one, huh?"

I smiled at his attempt at humor over his situation. After all, humor was how I dealt with everything. But my heart hurt at the fact that someone had hurt him. It was bad enough that his ex-wife had hurt him. The thought that some other idiot girl had done the same really pissed me off. From the things he told me, the man had spent most of his life feeling abandoned, betrayed, and left. Why? Could no one see the beauty that was in front of them? Were they blind to the complete complex wonder and creative greatness that was his mind and the glowing radiance that was his heart and soul? Seriously, I'd known Deaven—*really* known him— for maybe about a month at this point, and I knew my life was never going to be the same. He had changed everything in such a short amount of time. No one ordinary could accomplish such a thing.

How could someone willingly turn their back on something so special? It made absolutely no sense to me. Deaven was the type of man all women claimed to want—considerate, kind, selfless. Not only that, he was also playful, fun, and possessed a depth of character I wondered if anyone could ever reach the bottom of. He really listened to people when they spoke, and he paid attention to things so many others wouldn't even think twice about. Who would want to toss him away? If I'd been the one he'd chosen—if I could ever be that lucky—I would have grabbed onto him and never let him go. I would have cherished him every day of my life. He was one of the good ones, and I hated that he had been treated so carelessly by those in his life who had claimed to love him.

"Well, she was a freakin' idiot," I grumbled, more to myself than to him, but he heard and smiled at me, then chuckled in an almost self-conscious manner. It was so opposite his usual cavalier confidence.

I cleared my throat and tried to get back on topic. "So, your ex-wife and the girl you were just talking about, those were your only two serious relationships?"

"Yeah, I've dated a lot of girls, but not many of them last too long. It's not like I try to be a player, even though that's what most people probably think. I know what I want, but I'm also kind of fickle a lot of the time...with everything. I don't see any sense in leading someone on if I don't feel like it's going to go anywhere."

An admirable quality, even if that same sense of fairness had caused him to squash a lot of hope that what the two of us shared would be anything past two people realizing someone else could understand them coupled with a side of physical attraction.

I tried not to think about that too much because, as insane as it seemed, the fact that Deaven and I may never be more than friends, that he may decide he never wanted a relationship, or worse yet, that he never wanted *me*, was a horrific stab to my battered heart.

I decided not to dwell on it for fear of becoming morose, and I attempted to lighten the subject. "Yeah, I've had about four relationships, but only two that were really serious. I'm sure people thought I was a player back in the day also, especially as a teenager. I was such a flirt and I had a list of guys I wanted to kiss before I graduated." I giggled.

"I've only kissed two girls," he stated. "My ex-wife and my ex-fiancée."

I stared at him in stunned shock. "Seriously?" What guy had only ever kissed two girls?

He shrugged. "Yeah. I don't know, maybe it's backwards, but to me, sex always seemed like…just sex. But kissing seems really intimate to me. I could have sex with a chick and that would be that, but kissing is something that should be special."

I continued to stare in bewilderment, thinking he sounded an awful lot like Julia Roberts in *Pretty Woman*. "So, how many girls have you had sex with then?"

"Only my ex-wife." He sounded slightly offended. Probably because he had the same belief system as me and didn't do premarital sex.

I was both surprised and impressed at the fact that such a charismatic, flirty guy had only kissed two girls, and his reasoning was insanely romantic, but I suddenly felt like a total ho-bag if we were looking at it from his perspective. At the same time, an evil voice in the back of my mind whispered to me, *I will be the next one that he kisses.*

And I was.

Not too much longer, as a matter of fact. During a night much like this one, full of laughter and conversation, in a moment of complete boldness and determination, I stole a kiss from him that he did not fight. Neither of us really said much about crossing that line, but Deaven and I started spending almost every weekend together after that.

And I knew regardless of his claim to not want a relationship, somewhere deep inside me, I was positive that it was him or no one. And I am nothing if not tenacious.

Chapter Eight

Four Months of Light

That summer was the most amazing, chaotic, and convoluted several months I had probably ever had. Knowing Deaven and being close to him had propelled me forward into a world of mayhem I had not been adequately prepared for—physically, emotionally, or mentally.

Weekends were spent one of three ways—climbing, hiking, or vegetating.

Rock climbing until I felt like my arms were going to fall off, especially when we climbed outdoors on actual rock faces instead of in the gym. There were a whole lot of beat up body parts, bruises the likes I'd never seen, scraped off skin, moaning, swearing, and me conquering feats of physical strength I didn't think I could manage.

Hiking until I felt like my legs were going to fall off, especially when the first hike he took me on—which also happened to be the first real hike I'd been on in years—was twelve miles long. I'm pretty sure Deaven thought I was going to drop dead on that one, as I was wheezing like I'd never worked out a day in my life and my leg muscles were protesting to the point of excruciating pain. I did make it to the summit, mind you. I told all the other people with us to go on ahead as I was seriously holding up the group, but I slowly and methodically made it, which earned me a "good job, beautiful girl," from Deaven, and a beer at the top. Those words from him, although so simple, made everything worth it.

Granted, Roseanne thought something horrible had happened when I stumbled my way up to my apartment, looking like death and walking like I was from the zombie apocalypse, and I could barely walk for about three days afterward, but I became addicted to hiking as much as I became addicted to climbing. The skeptical part of me said it was more like I was becoming addicted to Deaven, and while that in itself was true, I found it more like I was just becoming addicted to life. Up until that point, I hadn't realized how much I'd only been surviving my life instead of living it.

There were people around us at all times, tons of new friends that overwhelmed me at first because I had been isolating myself for so long. I started out introverted, only speaking when being spoken to and sticking close to Deaven because he was the only one I was really comfortable with, but over the course of the summer, the walls I had so carefully constructed to keep the world out started to dissolve. It wasn't this dramatic event like you read about in fiction. It was more subtle, a quiet chipping away that no one was even doing intentionally. Deaven's friends were just like him—accepting, full of life, not what I had grown accustomed to in my experience with people. I was used to being weighed, measured, and judged. No one did that amongst Deaven's friends. I felt like one of the group for the first time in ages. And that feeling was just as addictive as everything else.

There were barbecues and nights out playing pool, friends visiting from out of town, pub crawls, plays, debauchery, dancing, so much beauty and light it made me feel starstruck and spellbound. And laughter. So much laughter. More laughter than I ever thought possible. Every time I did something with Deaven, I remembered what happiness felt like, and I realized how long it had been since I had really felt it. Even in times when I thought I'd been happy, I saw I had only been content. The kind of happy I felt with Deaven was the kind I'd last felt when I'd been a teenager, when I'd been writing and doing theatre and playing in the orchestra. When I had been running in every possible direction at once, juggling life, romance, friends. Before I'd become stagnant. Before I'd become ruined. Before I'd become this husk of a once great person.

The fear was always present, the cautious voice telling me it was all going to end in a burning ball of crap that would hurt me way worse than anything else thus far. It would tell me I needed to get away while I could, that I needed to return to my safe world. My prison.

I ignored it. I didn't care. Maybe it would hurt. I would survive. I didn't care if it all ended. At this point, I just wanted to feel something again. The risk was worth it. Deaven was worth it.

And while I loved all of the adventures we had as weekend warriors, my favorite times with him were the ones we spent just the two of us, vegetating on the couch watching movies and talking. Getting to know him was what intrigued me the most, for he had more layers and more colors and shades to his complex character than I could even name.

We would cuddle a lot of the time, both of us craving the physical affection we felt we had been denied for too long. He still held fast to his claim to not want a relationship, regardless of the fact that we already acted like we were in one, and I fell a little more every time I was with him. I wasn't shy about telling him this either. If he was going to be brutally honest, so was I. I had decided by now that, whatever happened, he was already my very best friend, and so long as he wanted it, that fact would always remain. I am and always have been fiercely loyal. Even if it ended up causing me pain, being his friend was something I would never willingly relinquish. I would gladly suffer knowing he didn't want to be with me the way I wanted to be with him if it meant he was still in my life. Life without Deaven seemed much too stark and cold to imagine.

But there were moments, small glimmers that kept me hoping we would one day become more than just friends who liked to snuggle and who flirted hopelessly. That and the overwhelmingly strong gut feeling that refused to be squelched by any amount of logic I tried to fire at it. No matter what I thought or tried to convince myself of, no matter how many times I tried to tell myself to get a grip and get over it, every time I was with Deaven, that feeling would just shoot back at me—*This is right. Just wait.*

Never in my life have I exerted so much patience. I didn't think I possessed the ability to be so patient. Every weekend I would leave his house frustrated and cynical, depressed at the fact that I couldn't have what I wanted, at least not all the way, and every weekend, I went back for more. Some would have thought it was masochistic. I just thought it was a means to and end, because no matter how frustrating it was, the thought that Deaven would be mine was always looping through my mind. Even when I wasn't actively thinking about it. It just seemed inevitable to me. I don't know why. I never have been able to place a finger on it. It just was.

For most of the summer, I felt like a girl with a hopeless crush, admiring him from afar like I did the rock stars I was enamored with, but there were times, quiet times, soft times, when I felt like he really was mine, if only for a small second. Times when he would let slip the rigid hold he had on his self-control and I saw a crack in the armor around his heart that was even more impressive than mine. I lived for those times.

Despite all of the turmoil I felt ninety percent of the time, we fell into a sort of comfortable pattern. The weekends were ours; it was an unspoken truth. All of our friends saw it, and told us as much. *"Deaven, Mickaela is perfect for you." "You guys are just the same!" "If anyone is your perfect match, it's Mickaela." "So...are you guys a couple or what? You spend all of your time together."* Words from friends all around who were curious, hopeful, and just confused. Deaven's response was always, "We're just friends," but I never let him know just how much those words eviscerated me every time he spoke them. He had to know, somewhere underneath his layers of protection, that we were already so much more than that...didn't he?

Or maybe I was just deluding myself. Maybe I really was just his BFF and that was the reason he always invited me everywhere he went and spent every weekend with me cuddling on the couch or having amazing adventures. It killed me to think this was true. That I was just "a bro." I'd been just "a bro" all my life, and it had never bothered me. I loved every single one of my guy friends. But I didn't want to be his bro. I wanted to be his girl.

You're a fool, the voice inside me said. *He is just going to play you like all the others. You're an easy mark, vulnerable and willing. He is using you to get what he wants, and then he will ditch you for someone prettier, wittier, far better...*

Oh how I abhorred that voice. And I argued with it frequently. Why go to all the trouble of being so painfully honest if his intention was to use me? And use me for what? We weren't even doing anything, so that made next to no sense.

My entire psyche was a jumbled disaster, and I had never been happier with it. Any moment spent with Deaven, no matter how confusing it was, was better than any moment I had spent...since I was maybe twelve.

It was on a random August night when I had the actual realization. I had been trying to deny it up until this point. But we had spent the evening listening to music at his place, discussing lyrics and the meanings behind them, then decided to go out into the foothills, away from city lights, and see if we could see the meteor shower that was supposed to happen.

We'd had difficulty getting to a place where we could be somewhat removed from civilization, and after bumping along a dirt road and almost ripping off the undercarriage of Deaven's car 4-wheeling over a ditch, we found ourselves sitting on the roof of his car, sharing a bottle of wine, and staring up at the night sky. The moon was full, making any start-gazing difficult, but it bathed the arid desert landscape in a silvery glow, making the North Valleys of our home suddenly seem like the set of a sci-fi movie.

A cool evening breeze blew over us, and Deaven sighed as he took a drink of wine. "You can already feel the weather change in the air," he said softly. "Fall is coming."

I glanced over at him, at the way the moonlight turned his blond hair more of a white shade and the shadows played across his profile. "I like fall," I stated.

He shook his head. "Not me. I hate winters here. I get depressed and it makes my back ache really bad."

Deaven had chronic pain from a back surgery he'd had as a teenager when someone at his job at the time had hit him with a forklift. I nodded in understanding, having been witness to times when his back was hurting him more than usual. "I can understand that. I don't really like winter either. I like the colors, though, of fall, when the leaves change. And I like to burn candles in my apartment and bundle up under blankets." I smiled at him, hoping to impart something positive into a subject that had suddenly turned him moody and sullen.

"Fall is the time when I always have something horrible happen to me," he muttered. "I hate it. And I hate being cold. I hate living here. I just want to leave."

He may as well have kicked me straight in the chest for the way the air left my lungs. I snatched the bottle of wine from him and took a long drink, trying to harness my sudden terror at the thought of him wandering off to his next location and leaving me all alone with only a memory of the light he had bestowed upon my life. I knew he had a wanderlust, an insatiable need to travel and discover. Couldn't he see that I had the same? That I wanted that too? That he didn't need to move to somewhere random; he could stay and find that there was good even in a place he didn't really care for, and there was a person who was more than willing to discover the entire universe with him...sitting right next to him?

He had been talking about moving somewhere else since I'd started hanging out with him, and it was a subject I usually tried to change as quickly as I could because I could not handle the thought of him disappearing on me. Because, let's face it, we all know that's what would have happened. And he would have claimed otherwise, saying that he would keep in touch and visit me, just like we all tell people when we relocate. I know firsthand how phone calls turn into text messages, and emails become "likes" on Facebook, and how visiting becomes something that happens maybe every other year if you're lucky. I knew there would never be a chance for Deaven and me to be anything other than "besties" if he were to move away. He would find some other girl who would catch his attention and distract him, some other girl who would be bad for him, who would hurt him, who would never appreciate him the way I could...

I scowled and took another healthy swallow of wine. "I used to hate it here too," I muttered. "But then I moved to Arizona and realized every place is just a place. Every place has good and bad. It's the people who matter." I knew he had lived elsewhere also; that wasn't my point. He was a smart man. I figured he could read between the lines.

"True, but the winters here just kill me. I want to go somewhere warmer, somewhere...else. I've posted my resume online. We'll see if I get any bites worth looking into. Arizona would be a nice place to live, maybe California...maybe Florida or New Orleans. I don't know."

I suddenly wanted to vomit, and my chest constricted to the point of pain. How could he possibly be so clueless? He had to know that his being so flip about this was murdering me. It made me feel like I was just some passing thing, that I didn't really matter at all, not even a friend worth sticking around for. Even though he constantly told me I understood him better than most, appreciated him more than most, that I was a "woman" in a world full of "little girls." I still wasn't worth sticking around for.

But then again, why would I think I *was* anything worth sticking around for? The only person in my life other than my mom who had stuck around for any length of time was Roseanne. I wasn't known for people falling over themselves to get to me. I had always associated myself with fire. Something that intrigued others, but once they drew near and got warm, they moved on. Getting any closer would be much too intense. It was the story of my freaking life.

Would I have to add Deaven to that list of passing beauty? Of people who came and went like the seasons, but never stayed more than one rotation? I couldn't handle it. Not this time.

"It's impossible to see anything out here," he said, breaking the suffocating silence. "I don't think we are going to be able to see any meteors, and it's getting cold."

"It's because the moon is full," I stated. "It's too bright. Let's go inside and just wait awhile. Maybe it will get better once the moon gets higher."

He pulled down his back seat and we crawled inside to where we could lie down and still see the sky out the back window.

"This is a cool car," I said as I situated myself. "It would be great for camping."

He made some sort of noncommittal noise at me and I sighed, lying back and staring out at the darkness in silence, trying to ignore the gigantic lump in my throat and the hollow feeling around my heart. In my mind, I could envision camping trips with him, sleeping in tents or the car or even out under the night sky. Laughter and bonfires and making love in the wild. My overactive imagination was sometimes my biggest curse.

"I love you, you know," I stated plainly. It wasn't really all that strange coming from me. I told all my friends I loved them, and told him frequently.

He turned his head to look at me. "I love you too...sometimes I think more than I've ever loved a woman... I just don't know what that means."

I glanced over at him, my eyes meeting his blue gaze. It always looked like there was so much going on behind that gaze. His mind was never quiet, rarely serene. I understood that in ways I would never be able to express to him. "Have you ever been in love before?" I asked.

He sighed and turned his attention back at the sky. "I thought I was, but now I realize I don't even know what love is, really. When I married my ex-wife, when I was with my ex-fiancée, I just wanted to be with someone. I've always wanted to be with someone, wanted to take care of someone. I thought if I found a partner, I'd be happy, but it's brought me nothing but misery. I feel like I've finally accepted being single, and strangely, that's because of you."

I stared at his profile for a few heartbeats of confusion before saying, "Huh?"

He smiled slightly. "I never thought I would find someone who could appreciate me, accept me, the way you do. Knowing you exist...somehow, it took away that need in me to find a partner. I'm okay being by myself. I'm okay with me because someone else is okay with me. I know it doesn't really make much sense. I'm trying to figure it out too. All I know is that I feel happy with my life for the first time in a long time...and I just want to keep that feeling."

That's because you're supposed to be with me, you moron! Oh how I wanted to scream that at him at that moment. Scream, *You're happy because you finally* did *find your freaking partner! Open your blind eyes!* And then I had the overwhelming desire to bludgeon him in the melon with some soap in a sock. So, my love and acceptance had taken *away* his desire for a relationship? Freaking great! The only reason that *didn't* damage my self-esteem in a way that could never be repaired was because I kinda-sorta understood what he meant.

I'd had people come into my life who had brightened it, who had taught me something about myself, who had made my entire existence better just because I'd known they existed, who had enabled me to make choices, do things, or feel better about myself just because of one phrase they'd said or one thing they'd done. So, I got where he was coming from in that way. And that was awesome. I was happy that I'd impacted his life in that manner since he'd exploded into mine like a cosmic storm.

But finding out that the "great lesson" I'd imparted on him was that he *didn't* need me was really not what I wanted to hear! I mean, don't get me wrong, I'm all for finding your independence. A person can't have a healthy relationship until they are measurably healthy as an individual. It was a good thing that he didn't need anyone else to be happy, and I was glad I had helped him realize that.

But...really? Come on!

"Finding your path is important, finding yourself even more so," I said instead. "Being totally fine with yourself is one of the biggest things you can realize. I'm glad you feel happy." *But where the hell do I fit into this equation?* I wished so badly that I could just blurt out my uncensored thoughts without sounding like a lunatic.

"I just don't know really what I want yet," he stated as if he had read my mind. "If I want to have someone, or if I want to just adventure alone. I like being able to do what I want when I want. I like not having to worry about someone else."

Touché. I couldn't argue with what I knew to be true of my own journey.

"I love hanging out with you. You're a lot of fun, and we share the most intriguing conversation. You're a great friend. Sometimes I think maybe I do love you, maybe I want to be with you, but how can I know for sure if I don't really know what love is?"

"Well, if you don't know what you want and you aren't sure how you feel, then what's the harm in giving us a shot?" *What?* Oh, okay. Apparently, I *could* blurt out my uncensored thoughts. That was good to know.

He glanced over at me and seemed to consider it for a few long, agonizing seconds, during which I berated myself nine ways from Sunday for having even opened my mouth. "I just don't want to lose you. If we didn't work out, I wouldn't want you to stop being my friend."

My heart softened and I let out a small sigh. "Deaven, you don't ever have to worry about that," I murmured. "I will never stop being your friend unless you make me." And that was so true it was painful. I know it sounded cliché, but it was complete one hundred percent truth. Having to go back to survival mode after he'd reminded me how to really live would be like being banished to a dark cave after dancing in the sun.

"I have concerns," he said. "Areas where I'm not sure if we would be compatible." His technical, logical mind was taking over any professions of his heart he may have uttered.

"Don't all people? You can't go into anything sure of it right away. No one can."

"I don't want to hurt you."

I lost myself in his eyes for a moment, and felt the weight of the conversation, the foreboding knowledge of what would undoubtedly happen. He was shooting us in the foot in his mind before he even gave us a chance. I knew it. I felt it. But I didn't care. "You're going to break my heart, aren't you?" I whispered.

"I might." Brutal truth. That was my Deaven. "I've always thought of myself as a lone wolf. Everyone sees me like I'm some kind of balloon that they like to play with, but they don't know that when they hold onto me too close, inside, I'm full of spikes."

I stared at him, studying the planes of his face, the depth of his eyes that had seen too much. I could see his heart there, in that moment. It was rare when he let me glimpse it fully, but it was extraordinary when he did. My own heart ached at the pain, the feelings of abandonment and betrayal he had felt in his life. He had prickles; so did I. Who didn't? Anyone who lived in this world had issues; we were all full of spikes. The only difference was that Deaven didn't hide his. He was who he was, and I loved him for that. I never had to wonder, never had to guess. Even if what he said to me wasn't what I wanted to hear, I knew it was honest.

I knew he was telling me the truth when he said that he didn't want to hurt me. He was the kindest man I had ever known, just confused...and more guarded than a maximum security prison despite his outgoing nature.

I knew I had to go for it, no matter how small of a chance it was. I had to take it or I would wonder forever. I knew I would be hurt. I just didn't care. "I'm a big girl," I stated.

He smiled, somewhat warily, and I scooted closer to him, not taking my eyes off of his. He closed the distance and kissed me softly, hesitantly. My heart jumped and rolled. Just that gentle pressure of his lips on mine turned me into molten liquid.

"I don't think we're going to see any stars tonight," he said, and just like that, his ice wall of protection went back up. I almost shivered from the chill.

"Yeah, probably not. The moon is too bright."

He stretched and rolled over onto his side, muttering that he was tired. I reached over and caressed his back with my fingertips, grazing them along his broad shoulders and studying the texture of his body. They drifted up his neck and twined softly through his hair.

He shivered and sighed. "I love the way you touch me," he murmured, his voice soft, husky. The twinge of vulnerability I heard in it made me want to take him in my arms and never let him go, but I knew that would make him feel trapped, especially given the conversation we had just had. Instead, I continued to run my hand along the contours of his back, and the realization of what I was feeling wrapped around me like a warm blanket.

It wasn't some crashing epiphany like I had anticipated, not a lightning bolt to the brain or an arrow to the heart. It was like a breath. Soft, subtle.

I was completely in love with this man.

Me, the person who had sworn off love and sealed my fate in my mind as the next crazy cat lady. The person who had wanted to vomit at the thought of ever opening my heart to another human being again. Here I was, handing it to an unsure man who probably was going to obliterate me. And I was doing it willingly.

Chris had been right. I just had to take the chance, be open to the possibility. Maybe it would end up hurting worse than I could even comprehend, but I knew it wouldn't kill me. And maybe that was why I wasn't afraid. I had already survived the death of a relationship I thought would be forever. I could live through this too if it went sour. Although, inside, I knew that getting over Deaven would be the most difficult hurdle yet, if getting over him was even possible.

But first things first, he was going to give us a shot. No sense in mourning something that hadn't died yet.

I tried to be elated as I knew I should be, but something just didn't feel right, and that feeling continued to ride along with us like some ugly elephant in the room for the next month or so. Our relationship felt forced, awkward. Deaven was even more reserved than he usually was, and I constantly felt like I was waiting for the other shoe to drop. Our natural chemistry felt off, and the tension was almost unbearable.

I went home from his house feeling confused and more hopeless than I had before we were together. I was constantly questioning myself, constantly wondering what I was doing wrong.

One weekend, he went out of town to visit his brother, and he barely spoke to me the entire time he was gone. The person who constantly text messaged me every day at his job when I'd been his "friend" barely acknowledged my existence while he was out of town when I was his "girlfriend." Even the times he did message me, he seemed annoyed, put out. It was exhausting to deal with, and I knew when he asked me to come over the day after he got back into town that something was amiss.

I was right. My gut was rarely ever wrong, and this time was no exception.

He'd bought me a bottle of my favorite wine in an attempt to soften the blow of his sudden decision to break up with me. All it did was make me want to retch. I couldn't drink when my heart was methodically being ripped into pieces.

"I think we should go back to just being friends," he said to me, while holding my hand. Even when he was hurting me, he tried to soothe me.

I heaved a sigh. "Yeah, I figured that was coming," I muttered. Strangely, in that first moment, I didn't feel the crushing pain. All I felt was drained. The pain came later.

"I just don't think we're compatible," he said.

I frowned at him, angry and hurt and freaking tired of feeling like a yo-yo. "How do you figure?" I practically spat. "We seem to have done just fine all this time, hanging out like every single day. Must be somewhat compatible in order to do that."

"Well, yeah, we are great as friends, but I don't think we are compatible as a couple."

"Why?" My word sounded like a bullet, hot and hard and fast. I was so done with beating around the bush.

He hedged a little, not really giving me an actual answer, before he finally said, "You have a lot of things that you need to deal with."

The burning anger welling inside of me almost thwarted the hurt. "And you don't?" Another bullet statement. Like *he* didn't have issues to climb his way through? I wasn't the only one trying to make sense of my life.

He nodded. "Yes, me too. We both do." He averted his eyes, and his shoulders slumped wearily. "I just don't think I can be what you need."

"How would you even know? You never even gave us a chance."

His gaze came back up to meet mine, hot with a flame of its own. "I did."

"Oh, did you? I didn't realize." I didn't care if I sounded like a bitch. Not at this moment.

"I told you I didn't know if we would work out."

"But Deaven, you never really gave us a chance!" I cried. "Not really. You had yourself convinced from the very beginning that this wasn't going to work. You never gave me a chance to prove to you whether your concerns about us were true or not. You think a month and a half is enough time to prove that? A month and a half of you freezing me out?"

"I haven't been freezing you out."

I arched my eyebrows at him and snorted, pulling my hand away. "You didn't believe in me, Deaven. Didn't believe I could be what you needed. You didn't believe in us at all."

He sat there like a stoic statue and I wanted to smack him and then shake him until his eyeballs fell out.

"I'm not what you need," he stated, more forcefully this time. "Every girl I've been with has told me that they feel like they aren't enough for me. It's only a matter of time before you feel the same way."

I was angry that he thought so little of himself, and angry that he had taken it upon himself to make a decision that wasn't his to make. "Oh, I *am* enough for you," I declared. He raised his eyebrows in faint surprise, and I wondered where that random surge of confidence had come from. "Besides, shouldn't that be *my* choice?" I spat. "How can *you* decide what is best for *me*? How can *you* decide what I need?" I shook my head and pierced him with my eyes. "You have no right to make that decision. You took a choice that was mine to make and you made it for me. Well, let me tell you something. You can't keep me from loving you. That is *my* choice. You have no control over that. And I *choose* to love you, whether you want me or not. Whether you like it or not. You can't *make* me get over you." For some reason, I felt like that was the ultimate defiance. I felt like he was trying to push me away, and this was me giving that self-preservation of his a great big middle finger. He could push all he wanted, but I was going to keep on loving him because I wanted to. I didn't want to not love him yet. It felt wrong.

He stared at me. He looked overwhelmed, and probably thought I'd lost my mind. "I'm not saying that there's no hope," he said. "Maybe we will end up together. I don't know. I need to get to know you better. Right now, all I know for sure is that I don't want to lose you as my friend."

Again with the friend thing. It was his one constant. At least I knew he wanted me around, but this dance was getting tiring. I tangled my fingers in my hair. My head hurt, and my heart was bleeding.

We talked more, said the same things and ran in the same circles. It always came back to the same thing. Deaven didn't know what he wanted, and that included me. He wanted things to stay the same, but without the "couple" title, more or less. There was no pressure that way. And whatever happened, happened. That was more the way I summed it up in my head than his words, but okay, whatever. I was too confused and hurt to care. Talking to him was probably like how Chris had felt talking to me two years prior. I was annoyed by the situation with Deaven, but how could I be angry with him when he was just dealing with his life the same way I'd dealt with mine? That would be all kinds of unfair. So I told him everything would be fine.

But I screamed at the top of my lungs when I got into my car. Screamed until my throat was raw. And I cried until I could hardly function. Horrible body-wracking sobs that robbed me of breath and made me feel like my chest was being ripped in two. I wasn't quite sure if I felt more heartbroken or more frustrated. It was kind of a toss up.

And still, underneath it all, the doubt, the anger, the pain, I felt it.

Just wait.

That voice that wouldn't go away. That feeling that wouldn't subside.

Just wait.

Wait for what? I wanted to scream. *Wait until I have nothing left of myself? Wait until my heart is just a piece of pulp that will never be salvaged? What am I even waiting for?*

I felt delusional and stupid, and nothing in my head or heart made any sense. It was all convoluted confusion, a storm of chaos that I couldn't sort out. Not right then anyway. All I knew for sure was that the aching, hollow hole in my heart when I went to sleep that night throbbed in a way that was almost unbearable.

That morning, Roseanne came over to get her spare key from me. Several weeks ago, she had found another place to live and was moving that day. I had completely forgotten. I stumbled to the door, in my pajamas and feeling like death, ripped the key off my key chain, and handed it to her.

"Why do I feel like we're breaking up?" she asked with a chuckle.

I gave her a meager smile while my heart twisted at her word choice. I hadn't told Roseanne about what happened. I couldn't bring myself to right then. I didn't even understand it myself. One part of me felt like it was all crashing down around me. The other part felt like nothing had really changed at all and that Deaven and I would still be together in the end. I didn't know which part to believe.

Later that week, I sat in my living room looking out the window at Roseanne's deserted, vacant apartment. It was strange not having her over there, lonely. I had gotten used to her constant company and conversation.

Earlier in the fall, my ex-husband had moved out of state and I had said a final goodbye to him. That had been strange as well, like closing a door to an old life.

My ex was gone.

Roseanne was gone.

I had Deaven still—sort of—but for how long?

The few remaining autumn leaves swirled around in the courtyard, and I knew a new season was upon me.

All I could think was that Deaven was right.

Winter sucked.

Chapter Nine

Choices of the Heart

The fall and winter ambled on as things always had been. Deaven remained aloof and guarded, except when he didn't. And I remained benched in the friend zone, except when I wasn't. If that confuses you, then you are getting the point. I remained steadfastly and maybe even stupidly loyal, ignoring my bleeding heart to the best of my ability, and when I couldn't ignore it, I just cried a lot in my bedroom.

I must have sworn about a hundred times—after I would come home from his house, or a night out laughing, playing, sharing, even making out now and again—that I was done. That I was quitting the entire thing and resigning myself to being just his friend. That I was killing myself slowly by allowing him the physical contact and the "friends but not" status. I needed to be firm, needed to be strong. I had to put my foot down and say enough was enough.

Every time I came to this decision, I felt like my resolve was unshakable.

And every time he smiled at me the next time I saw him, it dissolved like wet tissue paper.

Still, even though I was in turmoil ninety-eight percent of the time, the moments I spent with him were worth every ounce of confusion, every second of self doubt, and every weekend I left with the dull ache in my heart. It may sound twisted. Hell, I can't really comprehend it, even now. All I knew was that even with the pain of not being able to be with him the way I wanted, I was happy. He built me up even as he caused me to crumble. He renewed my strength even though my heart felt weak.

He never caused me pain on purpose. In fact, when we did have the heart-to-heart conversations where I blurted out all of my thoughts and feelings with no sensor and with enough tears that he probably needed a kayak, he held me, he cried with me, he wiped and kissed away those tears. Because he hated that he caused me to hurt. He hated that my heart was in a constant state of flux because he was confused. He told me countless times that he didn't want to lose me. Amidst the nauseating conversations about him relocating, traveling the world by himself, living it up bachelor style with his best guy friend, or whatever whim he came up with depending on which way the wind blew, he told me he loved me, that he still wasn't sure about us, that there was still hope.

I lived for that hope.

And the constant, somewhat nagging if still encouraging voice in my head that whispered, *Just wait.*

I know some people, actually a lot of people, who would say he was leading me on, dangling a carrot because he wanted me but not the commitment. That everything was on his terms. That I was whipped, pathetic, a lovesick fool who was desperately hoping for a miracle that would never happen.

But they aren't me. And they did not see what I saw or experience what I experienced. They were not granted per-mission to see the golden glimpses of his heart, the depth and beauty that lay beneath his exterior charm and charis-ma. Everyone loved Deaven, but very few people *saw* Deaven. I saw him. I saw he was like me. I knew his heart wanted mine, even if he hadn't figured it out yet. I knew it because his heart sang the same song as mine. The same tired, beat up, jaded, yet somehow still hopeful, disjointed, misunderstood, chaotic song.

I didn't care if the whole world thought I was insane. It was as I had told him before. I *chose* to love him. And in choosing to do so, I accepted the heartache that came with knowing I could not have him. It was my doing, and I would not hold him responsible for a choice *I* had made when all he had ever done was be honest with me. I would not punish him for going on his own life journey. Not when I was still in the midst of my own.

In this world, in this life, there are many things that try us and break us, many things that run us over and leave us befuddled and wondering where to go next. There are times when you feel like you no longer know the person looking back at you in the mirror. Some people never do figure that out. Others make up a life and an identity for themselves based upon what others think they should do or be. And others still are constantly self-evaluating, constantly looking for ways to better themselves, constantly questioning their choices, the paths they have taken, in an effort to figure out what in the world they are going to do with their future. If you're lucky, really lucky, sometimes you come to a point where you can say, "This is who I am. I am all my strengths and all my faults. I am all my bad mistakes and all my failed attempts, and I am also all of my greatest successes. This is me, for better or worse, and I *like* this person."

Deaven gave me that. He gave me that last piece of the puzzle I was looking for to make myself whole again. He gave me acceptance after years of knowing only rejection and belittlement. He gave me validation. He gave me strength to be crazy in all its forms, and he gave me the confidence to embrace that craziness. He gave me myself back, helped me find that elusive path I had been searching for.

How could I not love him for that?

And how could I stand in his way of finding the same for himself?

I couldn't.

I wouldn't.

And so it remained.

There are times when things really are just are what they are, and this was such a case. I loved Deaven. Deaven loved me; he just wasn't sure what that encompassed, and regardless of everything, we were best friends. That's just how it was. My heart chose to accept this, as much as it pained me.

And that was how I found myself with him in Sacramento, California in February.

January had been amazing; I won't lie. Mom and I had gone to Los Angeles to see our favorite metal band—because my mom really is *that* cool. It had been a much needed getaway, full of random adventure, good music, and relaxation. The whole time, Deaven had texted me nonstop. I tried not to think of that and equate it with the way I had attempted to text him when he had gone to visit his brother in Sacramento before he "broke up with me," and I had only been met with hostility. I was usually never the one to cast the first stone...

...Unless I was...but let's face it, my entire life was suddenly full of contradictions.

So, during sunset on Venice Beach, eating an overpriced cheese plate and drinking an overpriced half bottle of wine and not caring one iota, Deaven—who was house-sitting for me at the time—tells me that he's left me a present, and if I figured it out, he would give me a $100 gift certificate to anywhere I wanted. Most girls would think that was motivation; I just wanted the surprise. So, even when on the way home from the airport, I thought it might be a scavenger hunt, I didn't text him to tell him as much. I wanted the surprise.

Surprise I got...and beer bottles with notes in them in my toilet, behind picture frames, in the cat box, under my pillow, in my shoe, and various other places. I didn't care. What mattered to me the most was that he had taken the time to give me a fun, silly experience to come home to, and on his last note in the bottle, he had signed XOXO. What kind of "best friend" signed that? Not any that I knew. Not even Chris.

So, I was fortified through January, and made it through February with the promise that I would be following Deaven to Sacramento for a concert, and afterward, he would go on up north to Canada on his pursuit of happiness. On his "walkabout," if you're Australian. That's what I thought of it as. A journey to find oneself. He needed it as much as anyone, and I would never deprive him of it, even if I wished I could go with him...even if I wished he wanted me to.

Regardless of my thoughts, I had a great time in Sacramento, even if I did feel like I was going to throw up for the entire first night.

It was difficult following Deaven when I wanted to be *with* him, and it was more difficult to stay at his friend's house when I knew she had a thing for him. Girls knew these kinds of things about other girls. I was not stupid. And while this one was nice to me, I still was not stupid.

The times I spent that day with Deaven, just him and me by ourselves, were great. My anxiety was absent, and there was no issue, but the times spent with others, I felt on high alert, to the point that I only slept about three hours that night.

When he came to pick me up that morning, I was barely functional, and I wanted to retch. I let him believe I had a hangover because that was easier than telling him the truth. The truth was I was petrified. He had me so confused by this point that I didn't know if I could be myself, or if I had to pretend. Nothing made sense to me anymore. It all had up to this point. Deaven had caused me to find myself, so being with Deaven made it make sense, but suddenly, that wasn't how it worked. Me being myself meant me being in love with him, but that made him feel pressured. So, I had to pretend, which I never had to do with Deaven and wasn't fooling anyone anyway. I knew what I felt. He knew what I felt. It was always hanging over us.

He had been my partner up till now, metaphorically holding my hand and helping me out of the last stages of my crumbled life to a new, better one. Suddenly, I was on my own...and Deaven felt chasms away from me.

Breakfast was torture. I wanted to puke like six times. I barely ate anything, and I took the rest to go. We got lost on the way to San Francisco. That was the most fun we had until we finally made it to the city, got lunch, and I got to drink a half a pitcher of sangria.

Needless to say, I felt a lot better after lunch, but I still didn't stop questioning things. We went to Haight-Ashbury, where Deaven and I wandered aimlessly through all kinds of stores, and I knew...I *knew*...even more than I already had, that he was the only one for me. Anyone else was not an option.

Any other option made me hostile.

It was Deaven or no one.

It sounds insane, but it was true.

My gut had never steered me wrong.

Just wait...

Half the time, my "gut" made me uncomfortable. While I was the tenacious sort, I was never the "stalker" sort, and that was how I was beginning to feel.

I needed to get a grip.

So I tried not to pay attention to the way Deaven held

onto me throughout the concert we had gone to see, tried to pawn it off on the fact that we were having a good time and we were away from everything that was stressful about life and our situation. Trips were escapes from reality, right? I didn't want to think about the way I had imagined all day. Imagined he was mine. It sounded creepy.

We were "friends" after all.

Friends.

My most hated word.

I wasn't usually the "friend" to the person I wanted. It was an experience I was not used to.

So, one of the best trips I had ever taken to San Francisco ended with me crying on the ride back to Sacramento. Deaven felt helpless, and tried to console me to the best of his ability, but I was not afraid of the tears. I had become closely acquainted with them. "I'm fine," I told him.

"You're crying," he stated, sounding slightly bewildered.

I shrugged. "Yeah, I do that." I wiped at my eyes, and felt the familiar weight on my heart that I had also grown accustomed to.

"Why are you crying?" he prodded.

I gave him a look that had to have said, *"Are you out of your mind?"* I snorted. "Well, gee, Deaven, I don't know. The same reason I always cry, I would imagine." He stared straight ahead, his eyes focused on the road, and I sighed. "I just had a lot of fun and it sucks that it has to end."

"Well, we will do other fun things."

Yeah. As friends.

I settled back against the seat, knowing he was grasping at ways to try and make me feel better. We both knew "it sucks that it has to end" had nothing to do with the trip.

It was silent for several excruciating seconds before he finally said, "I just feel bad."

I glanced back over at him, at the highway lights highlighting his profile through the window. "Why?"

"Because...I know you want to be my girl, and I can't give you that right now."

The stabbing sensation was also familiar, and I turned my attention to stare back through the windshield. "I know," I said flatly. "You've told me. It's fine. But you know I love you. I have never hidden that from you, and I'm not going to start now. So, you're going to just have to deal with me being emotional about this if you want me to remain your close friend like you asked. Just let me cry."

The car fell back into silence, and before I could really comprehend much else, the exhaustion of the past twenty-four hours caught up with me, and I fell asleep like a dead person.

When I woke up, I was disoriented and confused, and it took me a second to realize we had arrived back at Deaven's friend's house where I was staying. My heart fell because I knew our trip was over. His would go on, but something new and strange had cropped up where the *just wait* thing was. I couldn't place what it was, but it felt sorrowful. It felt like finality.

I felt the tears burn again and I turned to Deaven before I got out of the car. "Can I please have a kiss?" I blurted. Maybe it sounded desperate, but it seemed of utmost importance to me at that moment. Like I just needed one more, to remember...

He seemed reluctant at first, probably because he was warring with his own self about making it seem like he was giving me false hope.

"Just one, Deaven," I whispered.

His blue eyes softened, and he reached over to cradle my face in his hand. He pressed his lips to mine, softly at first, then deepened the kiss to the point that my head spun. I cherished his lips in that moment, for a forlorn part of me felt like it may be the last time they touched mine. I could feel Deaven pulling away from me, and no matter how hard I tried to grip onto him, he just retreated that much further. There came a point where I had to just let go.

He walked me to his friend's door and made sure I got in all right, then drove away into the night. I knew he was just going to Canada, just going on vacation, but it felt much more symbolic to me. It felt like he was driving right out of the chapter of my life he had helped write.

Was I ready to face life without him by my side when he was the one who had made it beautiful again?

...Yes.

Yes.

Yes, I was.

That bewildered me as much as it leveled me. It was a weird mix of emotions. I knew that the good Deaven had brought to my life would remain even if he didn't, or even if our relationship changed permanently. I knew I would not retreat back into the dark hole I had crawled out of. I knew that from here on out, I was healed.

...I was whole.

I would be fine.

But I didn't *want* to be fine without him.

It was the want that mattered.

I didn't *need* Deaven. I *wanted* Deaven.

It may seem strange, but knowing that difference was profound. I had felt like half a woman, a crippled person, since I'd left my ex-husband and moved into my studio. I didn't anymore. Deaven had helped me with that, but he hadn't been the only one. My mom had helped me by being stalwart and strong, as she had been my whole life, my lighthouse amidst troubled waters. Lord knew where I would have been without that woman.

Chris had helped me by reminding me I could still laugh, that I could still party, that I could be ridiculous and do spontaneous things like walk around in the snow at night, and he had helped me not shut the door completely on love because of his faithful love for me.

Roseanne had helped me by showing me how awesome single life can be, how free and liberating. How no one should feel dependant on another. How being comfortable with yourself, and comfortable *by* yourself, are life lessons everyone should learn.

Deaven had been the sunrise that had lit up all of those truths I had learned. He had been the final piece. His presence in my life had taken all of the things I had come to realize and caused them to explode into a kind of rebirth. I was no longer broken. I remembered who I was, who I had been, and I was confident with that person. I *liked* that person. All the awkwardness, the self-deprecating, the second-guessing, the hiding...it was gone. I was not a woman who had lived through a divorce.

I was a woman who was living her life.

And I would live it regardless of whether or not Deaven was mine.

I didn't *need* him.

I *wanted* him.

Knowing that made the pain of it all bearable, and a bittersweet acceptance came over me. I only wanted him if he wanted me too. I deserved that. Until that happened—if it ever happened—I was going to be okay.

I would be okay.

At that moment, my heart still chose to love him, but I knew it wouldn't choose that forever. Forever is a long time to love someone who cannot love you back.

I probably slept worse that night than the night before, despite my epiphanies, and I don't know how I made it back home in one piece without falling asleep at the wheel. But I did, and crashing into my bed in my apartment felt like heaven. It was one of the few moments when I didn't even care about what Deaven was doing or where he was. I just wanted to sleep.

I didn't really expect to hear from him anyway. He was off on his epic vacation, and I had resigned myself to the fact that I was not going to text him unless he texted me first. If he wanted to talk to me, he knew where I was. I was growing weary of chasing after him. It was like trying to harness the wind. He knew I was here. I wasn't going anywhere. If he wanted me, if he missed me, he could come to me for once.

He texted me all the way up to Portland, Oregon, which surprised me. I figured he would relish the fact that he was away from me and the confusion I seemed to represent. But he continued to text me, and he called me during his last leg onto Seattle.

When he crossed over the Canada border, I knew he wouldn't be in range to text message me anymore, but I was shocked to see an email from him later that day, and then another one the next day, and one every day he was in Canada summarizing his trip for me.

I went about my life, doing my thing with surprisingly little heartache and pining, and was glad that he was having such a nice time. I was surprised again when he called me on his journey home. We talked for about two hours, about nothing really, and I wondered not for the first time if he realized that I was the one he was always making an effort to call, to email, to text. Didn't he see how much he was priori-

tizing me? That couldn't mean nothing. His actions ran con-
tradictory to his words.

When he finally returned home, he invited me over to see
his trip pictures and to tell me about everything that had
happened. I had gotten the cliff note emails, but I wanted to
hear about his trip in the way only Deaven could tell a story.

We had a nice time, and I enjoyed hearing about his adventures, but I did not enjoy hearing about the umpteen billion women who had apparently wanted him while he was
there. It irritated me that he would even tell me about that,
knowing how I felt about him.

And that was a first for me.

I wasn't sad. I wasn't heartbroken.

I was freaking irritated.

I was fed up, and I felt a shift within myself. I went home
in turmoil, and the next few weeks, I felt like I was counting
down to something, a breakdown or an explosion. I wasn't
sure. But I started to feel stuck and suffocated. I felt like the
walls were closing in on me, like I had to get out, get away. I
wasn't sure what I was trying to get away from, but I needed
to escape.

During one day that was particularly bad, I decided I
would take a jog around my neighborhood, as it was something that usually calmed me down when I was feeling restless. I started running, and I kept running. I ran harder and
further than I ever had, and had I been in better shape, I may
have pulled a *Forrest Gump* and run across the entire freaking
country. It seemed as if there was no possible way I could run
enough to lessen the tumultuous chaos inside of me.

The song on my MP3 player wasn't helping, and I suddenly relived every moment I had spent with Deaven since
meeting him. Every laugh, every drink, every game of pool,
every meal, every random adventure, every deep conversation, every kiss, every cruel word, every misunderstanding,
every hug, every success, and every failure. Like a movie
montage, I relived our entire weird relationship in a three-
minute span of time, ending with his gorgeous smile that had
lit up my world and would be the end of me.

Somewhere within my heart, I felt like something deto-
nated. It moved through me like a backdraft, a fireball cours-
ing throughout my body. I stopped running and bent over,

putting my hands on my knees and heaving body-wracking sobs that threatened to steal my sanity.

I couldn't do this anymore.

I couldn't continue to love a man who didn't know if he could love me.

I deserved more. I deserved love. I deserved a man's whole heart, not just pieces of it. I was better than that. I knew that now. It killed me, but I knew it.

I couldn't keep on playing this game with Deaven. He was never going to call an end to it because he didn't want to hurt me worse than he had.

So I had to.

I had to be the one.

I had to be the one to end it all.

Just wait was a falsity.

I didn't know when, but I cried because I knew regardless of the day or the time, it was going to have to be me.

It was strange when it happened.

I was at his house, on a weekend like any other. We were watching a movie, cuddling on the couch like we always did. I was behind him, trailing my fingers across his back and shoulders like he liked. The show had ended and there was about fifteen minutes of silence before I said it.

I studied the contours of his body, the curve of his neck. I breathed in the scent of him, sheltered it in my memory. I imprinted the way his strong body felt against mine, how safe I felt when I was close to him. I logged it all and locked it all away.

What was strange was that it wasn't dramatic, wasn't huge. It was quiet, like a sigh. A weary sigh.

"Deaven, I can't do this anymore."

One heartbeat of silence...

Two...

"I know I have to let you go," I continued.

I heard his breathing accelerate, and I continued to trace my fingers along his back while everything within my heart concerning him methodically shut down like an industrial plant powering off.

"I just don't think I can be what you need," he finally

said.

I gave a small, tired smile that he couldn't see, and nodded. "I know. It's okay." I couldn't fight with him anymore. All we did was run in circles. "I will always be your friend. Always." One more caress of my fingers down his arm and I stopped. I surrendered. "I'm going to Tahoe in a couple weeks," I told him. "I have to get away from here for awhile." Tahoe was about an hour away from where we lived, and I had decided after my run that I needed to escape. I needed out of my town so I could think, so I could process, so I could come to terms with not having Deaven, and let him go.

It was time to let him go.

He was quieter than I had anticipated, more introspective as well. I had thought he would seem relieved that I had finally let him off the hook, had finally just let him be. His reaction didn't make sense to me, but I honestly couldn't bring myself to care. I was emotionally and mentally exhausted. My heart was finished. It needed a break. It needed a vacation. And I was going to give it that.

Chapter Ten

Completely Unsuspected Surprises

Realized During Movies and Conversations about Dinosaurs

Deaven and I were fans of the film director/producer/writer Quentin Tarantino, who has brought us all such gems as *Kill Bill, Pulp Fiction, Jackie Brown*, and others. Even after my sudden realization I could not continue on in the fashion I had been going, we still got together every weekend. He was my best friend, after all. Maybe the best I'd ever had. I would never give that up.

The pain of knowing he wasn't going to be mine had subsided considerably, and I felt a certain peace when I was around Deaven now. The anguish and uncertainty were gone, the constant second-guessing and reading into everything. Now, it was just me hanging out with my buddy.

Did I love him still?

Of course I did. But it was on the backburner. I had a life to live.

I was proud of myself for staying on my side of the couch. Throughout the entirety of *From Dusk Till Dawn,* a Quentin Tarantino classic, I had remained on my end, not initiating cuddling or touching of any kind. While I enjoyed the physical affection, I was afraid it would launch me right back to where I had just gotten out of. I needed to be clear-headed about us. I needed to face this. If I was just going to be his friend, I needed to act that way. No more muddying the waters.

We laughed and talked like we had when we'd first met,

before things had gotten weird, and I found myself enjoying the new turn in our relationship. It would take awhile, but I could get used to this new me and Deaven.

I went to the bathroom, then came back and finished the movie. Afterwards, we got into a long, drawn-out theological conversation. I loved those kinds of conversations with Deaven. I couldn't have them with many people, and theorizing with someone of his intellect who had the same opinions as me was refreshing.

I'm not sure how long the conversation went on. All I know was that I had laid down on the couch and was thoroughly enjoying myself when out of random nowhere, Deaven said to me, "I want you to be my girlfriend again."

I think time stopped. Like, quite literally. I stared at him, and counted the heartbeats that happened in the silence to follow.

Then, I screwed up my face and cried, "What the hell?" Not the classiest thing to say following a declaration I'd been longing for, but it's what happened nonetheless.

He chuckled and scooted closer to me on the couch. He reached out for my hand, and I gave it to him numbly. "I think about you all the time," he said. "I know things have been weird, and I know you're going to Tahoe this weekend. If you end up finding some guy that sweeps you off your feet and you want to be with him over me, I get it, and I will concede defeat like a gentleman, but if you still want to be with me…I'd really like to give it a shot."

"Why?" I all but shouted.

He smiled. "Because you're insanely loyal, and I have fun with you, and we have the best conversation."

I shook my head. That answer was not satisfactory. "Why?" I repeated. I seemed to be stuck.

Deaven's expression was amused and there was mischief lighting his blue gaze. I narrowed my eyes and folded my arms across my chest. The butthead was actually mocking me.

"Where did this come from? What changed? You told me we weren't compatible." I prodded.

"I told you I didn't *know* if we were compatible."

"And you know now?"

"More or less."

I kept staring at him like he'd lost his mind. Maybe I'd lost mine. Maybe this entire thing was a hallucination. "Why?" I repeated.

He laughed and reached out to run his hands down my shoulders. "Because I really do love you, and I can see a future with you, if you still want that. I just had to figure it all out. I have never been close friends with a woman I've dated before. It was new territory for me, and I was so afraid that if we didn't work out, I would lose you, and I didn't want that to happen. I needed to make sure we weren't just physically attracted to one another, that we had a real foundation."

"I thought you didn't want a relationship."

"I didn't know if I did."

"I thought you wanted to move away from here."

"I do, but not right now. I'm fine here for now." He reached for my hand again and held it gently. His words were simple, but the look in his eyes said so much more. He was fine here because he knew I wanted to stay here. He was fine here because I was here.

I looked around the room. "Seriously, where are the hidden cameras?"

He squeezed my hand and gave it a little shake. "I thought I conveyed to you when we broke up that I just needed more time to think and sort things out."

The expression I gave him had to have reflected the weirdly pained rotating shock-joy-shock I was feeling. "No...that didn't really come across that clearly," I stated. He had sounded pretty final to me. The little nugget of hope he had tossed my way I'd figured had been to soften the blow. I didn't know that all this time he'd been saying variations of "It's not going to happen," he was actually thinking, "It totally might happen."

"Well, that's what I meant," he said. "I'm sorry, I was nervous."

Deaven? *Deaven* was nervous? Talking to me about matters of the heart made calm, rational, logical Deaven *nervous*? *I* had made him nervous? All this time I'd spent anguishing over my own muddled feelings, thinking he was impervious to them. Apparently, he was just quieter about it than I was.

I continued to stare at him, then glanced down at his

tumbler of tequila. "You're drunk," I stated.

He glanced at it too. "No, I'm really not," he said.

I snorted, trying to be flip even as every resolve I had made started to dissolve. "Okay, then ask me again tomorrow."

He gave me a wicked smile and leaned closer to me. "Okay." He breathed it in a way that said to me he knew I was full of it, that I was trying to be tough when he knew I just wanted to scream in elation.

My heart and mind warred for all of two seconds before my heart told my mind to cram it up its ass, and I surrendered to his kiss and the make out session that people only read about in romance novels.

What followed was surreal. Several days of Deaven being the attentive boyfriend, and kissing me goodbye as I went off to Tahoe for my retreat.

What had been a getaway to get over Deaven became a getaway to understand exactly what had happened with Deaven. Maybe it was because I had pulled away. Perhaps the lack of pressure had done the trick. Or maybe it was just as he said. He couldn't stop thinking about me and really had just needed to sort it all out in his mind and heart. Maybe it had worn him thin, had made him realize I could match him in every way.

Maybe I had fallen into a worm hole and was actually in an alternate universe.

I don't know. All I know was that Tahoe taught me several things.

#1. Sometimes, traveling by yourself is completely needed and necessary.

#2. Confronting your past and embracing the unknowns of your future is liberating.

#3. I loved Deaven, and I was his...because I had always been his. Apparently, he had never lost me at all.

The next several months were a whirlwind of activity, and all I know is that once Deaven decided to commit, he did so all the way. Any doubt he may have had, any question, any concern, vanished. He dove ahead full bore into our relationship to the point that it made my head spin.

He started telling everyone we were together, which was the complete opposite of his hush-hush attitude the first time around. I was invited to family dinners. He was never shy with displays of affection in front of others. In fact, he was constantly at my side, holding my hand, playing with my hair, putting his arm around me, kissing me on the cheek as he walked by, little things that meant everything to me. I felt like I was nestled into the warmth of his heart for the first time, and if I had loved him before, the sense of belonging and adoration I felt for him now made that first love seem small. Being truly loved by Deaven was better than I had imagined it could be, and I had done my share of imagining.

Those months of spring and summer when I'd met Deaven, while full of beauty and light, felt dwarfed by the fiery blaze of being truly his and knowing he was truly mine as we made our way into a new spring.

It was hard to believe I had been with him in some fashion for an entire year. A year of tumult and insanity, joy and sorrow, laughter and chaos and tears. All of the doubts we both had seemed to melt like the snow on the mountains, and the winter my heart had known made way for the warmth of the sun.

It was on a warm night in June when we were lounging on his couch. We were watching *Kill Bill*, even though we had seen it many times before. Deaven had asked me if I wanted to go have dinner in the park with him tomorrow night, and the way he had asked me had made me sick to my stomach for half a second. I got that foreshadowing feeling that something big was going to happen, and I didn't think I could live through another bottle of my favorite wine to soften to blow of him totaling my heart.

I told myself my fears were unfounded. He wasn't acting strange or like he was about to drop a bomb on me. We hadn't had one fight or argument since we'd become a legitimate couple, and he had told me just the other day, while enfolding me in his warm embrace, that he was very happy with the way our relationship was working out.

Halfway through the movie, Deaven and I started having one of our trademark epic conversations. We started talking about religion, and somehow that conversation turned into one about dinosaurs. What it would be like if dinosaurs still existed, but didn't eat people. Would it be like *The Flinstones*? Would they be our work animals? This conversation went on for about an hour's worth of speculation.

Sometimes, we were complete geeks, and I loved every minute of it.

When the conversation finally wound down, Deaven fixed me with a look that made me nervous. He gave me an impish smile and said, "I have a surprise for you tomorrow."

I raised my eyebrow and tried to play it cool while my stomach started to churn. "Oh yeah?"

He nodded and ran his hand up my leg to my knee, as I was sitting with my legs on his lap. "If you guess it, I'll give it to you early."

I rolled my eyes playfully and stood up because I had to go to the bathroom. "What, you going to propose to me?" I mocked. I knew that was never going to happen. At least not for awhile. That was probably way too much to hope for anyway. The terrified part of me still lived in fear of us having an expiration date. "I have to pee," I stated. "I'll be right back."

I didn't even dwell on what his actual surprise might be. My fears of him breaking up with me were unfounded in this instance. I doubt he would have been teasing me about it and trying to make me guess if that's what it was. Maybe he had gotten me a nice necklace or something. Or concert tickets somewhere. That would be awesome.

When I went back into his room, Deaven was still sitting there with that mischievous smirk. I raised my eyebrow in question and smiled, then straddled his lap playfully and messed with his hair. "What is with you anyway?" I giggled.

He shrugged. "Well, you guessed it, so I have to honor it now."

I frowned, and before I could even formulate any kind of thought, he slipped a ring onto the pinky finger of my right hand.

"Will you marry me?"

My heart slammed into my ribcage so hard I almost passed out. I blinked down at the ring and my vision swam for a second. Every single thought I may have been having fled my mind save one.

"Wh-what the hell?" He laughed, and I looked up at him. "Why is it that my answer to the two most important questions you've ever asked me has been 'what the hell'?" My brow furrowed. "And why were both times when we were watching Quentin Tarantino movies?" I was babbling.

Deaven laughed again and reached up to smooth the hair away from my face. "Is that a yes?"

I looked back down at the ring and shook my head. "Well, first of all, you put it on the wrong hand." I gave him a look, teasing him in order to buy myself time to get it together before I fainted. "And it's on my pinky finger."

He shrugged nonchalantly. "I don't know what I'm doing." His tone was indifferent, but I knew better than to think he was feeling nothing. Deaven was rarely feeling nothing. Even if he came across icy at times, I knew an inferno burned inside of him. He was just very good at keeping all those passionate feelings hidden.

I slipped the ring onto my left hand, admiring the intricate metal work of the band. It looked like a vine, with tiny rubies sparkling throughout it. Not the traditional engagement ring. It was exactly what he knew I would like. "It's too big," I stated, holding my hand up.

He frowned. "Well, crap."

I giggled, and some kind of sense finally returned to me. Deaven had just asked me to marry him. My head swam with the knowledge that my greatest fantasy had just come true, and here I was being silly and snarky because the information was having trouble computing.

"I can have it resized...if this means you're accepting." Deaven gave me a pointed look.

A slow grin spread across my lips and I wrapped my arms around his shoulders. I buried my face against his neck and closed my eyes. "Of course it's yes," I whispered. "It's always been yes."

He held me close and we stayed like that for a little while as I willed my heart to try and beat normally so that I could take a full breath. A million things were whirling around and colliding in my mind. I was going to be Deaven's wife. It was everything I had wanted, and it frightened me so amazingly that I was almost paralyzed by it. It was the ultimate leap of faith after my last marriage had failed so enormously. What if this time was the same? What if Deaven decided he didn't want me anymore after awhile? What if he thought he'd made a giant mistake and that we weren't compatible after all? What if...?

Stop it, Mickaela. You know this is right. You've always known this is right. Why are you questioning your happy ending? Not everything beautiful in life dies. Not everything you build comes crashing down.

I sighed, and did my best to quiet my thoughts. There was no way any one person could have all the answers for every what if in a situation. There were always a thousand what ifs, and a thousand possibilities of both success and failure. Sometimes, you just had to take the chance.

"I'm scared," I murmured.

Deaven moved so that he could see my face, and he frowned in concern. "Why?"

I shrugged. "Scared you'll change your mind."

His eyes softened and he tucked a strand of hair behind my ear. "I'm not going to change my mind, Mickaela."

"You don't think this is too soon?"

He smirked. "Too soon? No. Let's face it, we both know we've basically been together this entire time. The only person I was fooling was myself."

I smiled, and warmth flooded my heart at his admission. So, I hadn't been completely crazy that whole time after all. The *just wait* had been valid.

"I have so much fun with you," he continued. "I love our relationship. We *are* compatible. We do make sense. We can have a good life together." He gazed into my eyes and I felt the weight of his words, the truth of them. I felt his beautiful heart. "Will you travel with me and have adventures with me?" He turned the full power of his magnificent grin on me. "Will you be there for all of the mayhem and all of the dinosaur conversations?"

The last shred of doubt I had incinerated, and overwhelming joy and love flooded me. This was my happily ever after. This man was my fictional hero come to life. This was my very own love story, complete with angst-filled plot and dark moment where the couple doesn't know if they will end up together.

This was where two people who had been broken were now only a little bit dented. This was where two people forged a new path not based upon the blunders and sadness of the past. This was where two people, slightly misunderstood, too creative to make sense, with volatile emotions that sometimes trumped reason, found their forever in each other.

This was where I kissed him.

All of the lingering what ifs were pushed aside to be dealt with at a later time. I didn't care about them. All I cared about was how the man holding me made me feel. He had always made me feel like I could fly. He had helped me re-member how to fly on my own, but it would be so much bet-ter soaring beside him.

Two phoenixes from their own ashes.

Like Chris had said.

I wondered if my friend was psychic, because he had been right all along.

Chapter Eleven

Home is Where the Heart Is

I was yanked out of my meandering thoughts by my phone blaring. I stopped my walk down memory lane and frowned at the clock. It was almost midnight. Who in the world was calling me at midnight? Deaven was working the graveyard shift at the hospital, and he never called me from work anyway. My mom was asleep.

I looked at my phone and my frown deepened when I saw it was Roseanne. I answered, and her tear-filled voice distracted me from my reminiscing as she told me about the nasty breakup she had just had with her boyfriend. I listened and tried to be as supportive as I could, even though I knew my words weren't going to make her feel any better at the moment.

Roseanne had thought this guy was the one, and she suddenly found her entire life dumped over on its head. There were no magical words that would make that any better right now. I knew that more than anyone. She would survive, but it was going to suck for awhile.

I did my best to console my sister-by-choice and when she finally got off the phone, I sighed and looked at the wedding picture of Deaven and me up on the shelf where I used to have a picture of me and my favorite rock star—he had been the only man in my life for a really long time there. I stared at the picture for a moment, then looked down at my wedding ring.

I was lucky.

Really, really lucky.

Not a day went by when I did not count my blessings for

what I had in my life.

Deaven and I had been married in September. We didn't want to wait. Now that all of the confusion was sorted out and we knew that what we really wanted in life was each other, we didn't want to sit on it. We wanted to start our life together.

So, of course, three months of complete drama ensued, as is expected. But we got through it with a little help from some amazing friends, and on the first day of fall—which was a complete coincidence—in a small, intimate ceremony in a rose garden, surrounded by family and close friends, Deaven and I became husband and wife.

I guess fall isn't such a terrible season after all.

We spent an extravagant week in San Francisco for our honeymoon. We hiked and explored, we ate and drank everything, we made love...a lot. It was perfect, all of it, even the weird and awkward moments. It was perfect because we were doing it all together.

Since Deaven had been living in his uncle's basement the entire time we had dated, we decided he would move into my studio until we could find a better place. It just made more sense, and while it was small, we would live, especially since I had basically converted it into a one-bedroom.

So, with the exception of his couch and his ginormous television, Deaven had left all of his worldly possessions at his uncle's and had moved into my little lair. We got through a winter of the closet gathering ten kinds of condensation and trying to mold all of his suits and dress shirts; we got through dos-a-doing around the bed in order to get into the bathroom and the closet in an attempt to both get ready for an event at the same time; we got through bleaching the mildew out of the bathroom that grew on the walls, ceiling, and every other available surface every three months; we got through being alternately roasted and frozen out of the shower because our water line connected with the other tenants; we made it through grilling meat on the floor like Native Americans because we had no counter space and only one electrical outlet.

We made it through Deaven's car being the unfortunate victim of a hit-and-run, which had caused another car to veer into the back end of his and smash it to bits.

We made it through the drug dealers who moved into the duplex in front of us.

And we made it through the crazy drunk guy who lived down the street who got into a fight with one of our neighbors, and in an intoxicated rage, had started throwing things at all of our apartments, and had taken a knife to our screen door.

It was a winter of interesting events.

But now, we were leaving this place that had been the symbol of my independence. We had made an offer on a condo, which had been accepted, and soon, all of this would be a distant memory.

I wasn't sure how I felt about that.

Of course I wanted to move into a bigger place that was more suited to two people, and have a home that Deaven and I felt was *ours* and not *mine*. We both still referred to the apartment as "mine," even though he lived here now. It seemed like he was squatting on my territory, and I didn't want him to feel that way. I wanted us to make a home that was his and mine together, not live in the place that had been my post-divorce hovel.

But despite all of that, despite knowing it was time to move on and put my studio behind me, I couldn't help but be a little bit sad at leaving it behind. It had been where so many monumental things had happened to me.

I had gotten divorced.

I had regained my sense of self.

I had proved to myself and others that I could make it on my own.

I had laughed with Chris, and invited a friend into my home and life for the first time since moving.

I had found meaningful employment that utilized my love of the written word.

I had kicked a man out of my apartment, which was so much more metaphoric than that simple act.

I had drank with Roseanne, and danced with feather boas, and listened to rock music until we both wanted to pass out from laughing and singing the lyrics. I had run over to her apartment to kill centipedes, and to help put out the fire when her oven had run too hot and burned the pizza she was cooking to a crisp.

I had met Deaven.

I had cuddled with him here, talked with him here, cried myself to sleep over him here.

This apartment had been my refuge and safe haven, my place of mischief and intrigue, my place of self-discovery.

I had found myself here.

It was hard to leave that behind, even though I knew I had to.

This apartment had been mine, had been my way of remembering who I was, had been my grounding point when things became too insane.

I didn't need the structure anymore, because I had Deaven. He was my strength. He was my reminder.

It was time to start a new chapter. The time of the studio apartment had come to an end.

I accepted this, even as it pained me. It only pained the nostalgic part of me. The rational part understood and embraced the future, the possibilities.

With a sigh, I prepared myself to go to sleep, even though it was strange doing so without my husband.

My husband...

It still boggled my mind to think I had him. He was my greatest gift, and I was so happy I had listened to my gut during that entire time of turmoil. He had been worth waiting for.

Ten years, I'd waited for him. I'd known it at eighteen, I just hadn't understood it. Was it luck?

No.

It was a blessing.

As I pulled the covers over me and prepared to sleep, my phone beeped one more time. I glanced at the text from Deaven that read, *Bad news, the deal for the condo fell through. I just checked my email. We're back to the drawing board.*

I stared at it for a second then started to laugh. Well, didn't that just figure?

I sighed as I lay back in bed and stared at the ceiling. Looked like we were going to have to deal with this small space for a little while longer. That was okay. It didn't matter. Home is where the heart is. And my heart had always been with Deaven.

Deaven was my home.

About the Author

Brieanna Robertson

If someone were to ask me what I am, it could be summed up in one, simple word: Dreamer. Ever since I was a small child my imagination has run wild. I have been telling stories for as long as I can remember, creating grand worlds in my head and going on adventures that were invisible to others around me. Am I eccentric? Yes. Am I proud of that? Absolutely.

I write about the things that inspire me, both in this world and in realms only seen with the imagination. My heroines are sassy and strong. My heroes are sometimes shy. I have an obsession with music (and musicians) and a fascination with wings. I believe true love does exist, and some-times it is found in the strangest, most unexpected places. I also believe that family and close friends are the glue that hold people together.

Above all things, I believe in being true to yourself and seizing the day. Life is an amazing gift. Make your experience as beautiful as you possibly can.